A Dangerous Business

A
DANGEROUS
BUSINESS

Michael Underwood

St. Martin's Press
New York

Library of Congress Cataloging-in-Publication Data

Underwood, Michael.
    A dangerous business / Michael Underwood.
      p.   cm.
    ISBN 0-312-05842-X
    I. Title.
    PR6055.V3D36   1991
    823'.914—dc20   90-29880
                                             CIP

First published in Great Britain by Macmillan London Limited.

First U.S. Edition: May 1991
10 9 8 7 6 5 4 3 2 1

A Dangerous Business

Chapter 1

Rosa's guidebook to Amsterdam informed her that Leidseplein was the 'most unrestrained square in Europe'. She was uncertain whether these should be read as words of encouragement or caution. One thing for sure, they did nothing to prepare her for the shock she received when walking there on their second day in the city.

It had been Peter Chen's idea that they should spend a long weekend in Amsterdam. It was April and he had recently returned from a lengthy stay in his native Hong Kong. Rosa had found it an enticing suggestion. Her previous knowledge of Holland was a bicycle trip through the tulip fields when she was a schoolgirl. Everyone had told her what a perfect country it was for cycling as there were no hills. What they had neglected to mention was that, no matter in which direction you pedalled, you'd be met by a head-on wind. Or so it had seemed at the time.

Peter clearly expected that, on his return, he and Rosa would take up where they had left off. They had known one another for several years and had been lovers for most of that time. Paradoxical as it might seem, he provided an element of emotional stability in her life.

Peter had made all the arrangements for their visit and they were staying in a small comfortable hotel overlooking a canal, not far from Leidsestraat.

'This evening we'll have a drink at the American Hotel,' he said, as they lay half-naked on top of their bed. The earlier part of the day had been spent in sightseeing under Peter's guidance and they were now recovering before

7

tackling the evening. 'It's art nouveau at its best,' he went on, 'or its most ghastly, according to one's taste. We might even have dinner there, but we needn't decide that yet.'

He turned his head and gave Rosa a kiss.

It was around six thirty when they set out to see what the rest of the day held in store. A short walk brought them to Leidseplein which presented an animated scene of pedestrians, weaving cyclists and trams charging from every direction.

'We'll sit outside,' Peter said as they approached the hotel.

'I doubt whether we'll find a table. It looks packed,' Rosa remarked.

'Leave it to me,' Peter said, advancing determinedly toward the rows of tables set out in front of the hotel.

Rosa, who had held back, let out a sudden gasp. 'Peter,' she hissed.

He turned and looked at her in surprise, then came back to where she was standing.

'What's wrong?'

'That man at the table in the second row. It's Eddie Ruding.'

Peter followed the direction of her gaze. 'You mean the table with the three men who are drinking beer?'

Rosa nodded. 'Ruding's the one on the right.'

Peter frowned. He recalled Rosa telling him of somebody called Ruding whom she had unsuccessfully defended on a burglary charge. It was a case that had presented her with a number of problems.

'I don't want him to see me,' she said, turning her back on the scene. 'He didn't look in my direction, did he?'

Peter shook his head. It seemed wiser not to mention that he had observed one of Ruding's companions staring at her.

'I thought you told me Ruding was sent to prison.'

'He got five years, so what on earth is he doing in Amsterdam? The trial was only a few weeks ago.'

8

'Either he's escaped, or it isn't Ruding at all.'

'If he'd escaped, there'd have been something in the papers. But I've not seen a word.'

Peter gave a helpless shrug. He had no wish for their weekend to be spoilt by the unexpected sighting of one of Rosa's clients. Moreover, he couldn't understand why she seemed so upset. Surprised yes, upset no.

Without further word, he steered her firmly to the farther side of the square and thence over the bridge in whose shadow many of the city's canal tours started. There was another large hotel across the street and, dodging the ubiquitous trams, he led Rosa to its café-bar.

'We'll have a drink here and go back to the American Hotel for dinner. We can use a side entrance and avoid the people sitting outside.' He gave Rosa's hand an affectionate squeeze. 'Relax. Forget Eddie Ruding.'

Rosa realised she must try and put the whole unsettling episode out of her mind, or at least not let it obsess her thoughts. She owed that to Peter. But seeing Eddie Ruding in Amsterdam when she believed him to be behind the bars of an English prison had left her with a feeling of disquiet. She was also determined to find out the truth.

After a couple of strong drinks, they walked back across the canal to the American Hotel and found their way to the restaurant where Peter persuaded the head waiter to give them a window table. Rosa felt as if she were in a goldfish bowl. After all, if she could look out, others could look in. The outside tables on the terrace were still fully occupied, though the one at which Ruding and his companions had been sitting was now taken by two girls and a youth. The girls were laughing uproariously while the youth sat looking glum. Waiters scurried between the tables bearing perilously laden trays.

Their food arrived, but Rosa continued to dart nervous glances about her. Peter, who had begun to eat, paused and stared at her with a worried expression.

'I've never seen you like this before,' he said. 'Why

are you so uptight? After all, would it really matter if Ruding did happen to see you? He'd probably have stood you a drink if he'd been given the chance. What is it you're afraid of?'

'I'm not afraid of anything,' she said with an attempt at a smile. 'It's just that seeing Eddie Ruding here has come as a shock. I can't explain it any more.'

The truth was that defending him had been a worrying experience and that she had been unable to dismiss the case from her mind during the weeks following his conviction. And now this had happened.

She put a hand across the table and placed it on Peter's.

'I'm sorry I'm being such a wimp. I've been looking forward to this weekend and I promise I won't let Eddie Ruding spoil it.'

By the time they had finished dinner, the street lights had come on, though there was still twilight. Neon signs around the square were working overtime confirming popular belief that advertisements for beer and airline flights look much the same in any language.

On leaving the restaurant, they turned in the direction of Leidsestraat. A five-minute walk would bring them to their hotel. The streets were thronged with Saturday evening crowds, through whose ranks cyclists skilfully wove their way.

They had walked about eighty yards when Peter gave Rosa's hand a tug and said, 'Let's go and look in that jeweller's window.'

It was a shop on the other side of the street with a mouth-watering display of precious stones. Rosa thought Peter might be intending to buy her something there before they returned home. But it was an extravagance she wouldn't permit. Even though she knew he could afford it, the puritan streak in her nature would never allow her to wear emeralds or sapphires the size of butter beans.

As he led her across the tramlines, she was aware of a tram bearing down on them from some thirty yards away.

She quickened her pace to pass in front of it, but was too late to notice a cyclist racing alongside it. The tram's warning bell sounded dementedly and she felt a sudden sharp jolt which sent her spinning to the ground. Time seemed to stand still and the next thing she recalled was looking up into the stricken face of the tram-driver who stood frozen at his controls.

'Are you all right, my darling?' Peter asked anxiously as he knelt beside her.

'I think so,' she said uncertainly.

A number of people had gathered round and helping hands raised her to her feet.

'It was that crazy cyclist,' an elderly man said. 'I think he suddenly realised it was you or him. A question of *sauve qui peut*, as they say in French.'

Rosa glanced up at the tram-driver who was now mopping his face. His expression was one in which relief was tinged with disbelief.

Peter put an arm around her and steered her gently into a shop doorway. He thanked everyone who had given a helping hand and assured them that they were close to their hotel. Rosa felt she owed it to the tram-driver to send him on his way with a smile. If he had not been alert and the tram had not been blessed with powerful brakes, it could have ended very differently. A childhood jingle came uninvited into her head and she began to giggle. Peter gave her a worried glance, as if expecting full-blooded hysterics.

'What made you giggle?' he asked when they were back in their hotel. 'You had me worried.'

'I suddenly thought of a silly rhyme my brother brought back from school one day. It used to send us into stitches. It ran, "Oh, look, mama, what is that mess that looks like strawberry jam? Hush, hush, my dear, it is papa, run over by a tram."'

Rosa had the impression that Peter found it as unamusing as her father had. He was suddenly at his most inscrutable and she wondered what was going through his mind. The

11

truth was that in the split second in which everything had happened he was under the strongest possible impression that the youth on the bicycle had deliberately pushed Rosa into the path of the tram.

There was only one person in Amsterdam who could have wished to arrange an accident of that nature and his name was Eddie Ruding.

When Rosa woke up the next morning she at first thought it was raining. Then she realised that the sound of splashing water came from the bathroom and that Peter was having a shower. He was the cleanest person she had ever met, showering not only morning and evening but often in the middle of the day as well.

She turned over and then wished she hadn't. Her left side was stiff and sore from shoulder to ankle. It was a miracle that nothing worse had befallen her. Trams might still retain an old-fashioned charm as they clattered and swayed on their preordained journeys, but they were not to be trifled with.

She was about to find a more comfortable position in which to lie when the bathroom door opened and Peter stood there wearing a pair of white briefs. His skin, as always, looked firm and smooth and healthy.

'Did I wake you up?' he asked.

'No, I'd just surfaced from a dream in which I was being chased by a tram. It was a relief to find that I wasn't.'

'Was I there?'

'You were driving it.'

'We'd better not try and analyse that.' He walked over to the window and drew back the curtains. The bedroom was immediately flooded with sunlight.

'What time is it?' Rosa asked.

'Just after eight. A bit too early for breakfast,' he said, slipping off his briefs and getting into bed beside her.

'What are the plans for today?'

12

'Depends on how you feel. I thought we'd postpone our visit to the van Gogh museum. You won't feel up to the rigours of a museum in your present state.' He ran a hand gently along her left thigh. 'Sore?'

'Yes.'

'How did you sleep?'

'Fitfully.'

'You weren't as restless as I'd expected.'

'By which you mean I didn't disturb your own sleep.' She drew a deep breath. 'You smell so fresh and clean that I must go and have a shower myself. Then let's have breakfast.'

'And a talk.'

'What are we going to talk about?' Rosa asked with a yawn as she prepared to get out of bed.

'Eddie Ruding. I want you to tell me everything about his case.'

'Why this sudden upsurge in interest?'

Peter reached for her hand. 'Because I'm sure the tram incident wasn't a mere accident. I think the youth on the bicycle tried to push you under it. It wasn't difficult to make it appear to be an accident.'

Rosa shook her head in bewilderment. 'But why should anyone want to push me under a tram?'

'The answer to that lies with Eddie Ruding.'

'But not even he has any reason to wish me dead.'

'That remains to be found out. Come on, I'll fix the shower for you.'

Startled by what Peter had told her, Rosa fell into deep thought and was hardly aware of taking the shower. If Peter was right, it meant that Ruding and his companions had not only spotted her, but had immediately realised that she posed a threat. At least, that was their supposition.

Neither before, during, nor after Eddie Ruding's trial, however, had she felt herself in any sort of danger. After he had been convicted, she had visited him in the cells before he was taken away to start his sentence. He was in a resigned, if

13

somewhat bitter mood, and Rosa hadn't lingered. They had shaken hands and that was that.

Now a mere six weeks later he was breathing the free air of Amsterdam.

Chapter 2

'Begin at the beginning,' Peter said across their breakfast tray. 'How did Ruding become your client in the first place?'

'I defended him about two years ago and, thanks to the police making a fine old mess of the case, he got off. So when he was in trouble again he came knocking on my door, believing I had a magic touch. On this occasion I had the impression from the outset that the powers that be weren't too pleased at my involvement.'

'Why not?'

'Because they didn't want a fight on their hands. They'd have preferred the case to be disposed of quietly and without fuss. There were aspects the authorities didn't want to have aired.' She paused and went on in a thoughtful tone. 'Eddie Ruding is a professional burglar in the prime of his criminal life. He has a Dutch father whom he told me he hadn't seen since he was a boy and an English mother who's one of those cockney matriarchs. He lives with her and they adore each other. He grew up in both countries, so it's not all that surprising to find him in Amsterdam.'

'Except that you thought he was in prison in England,' Peter broke in.

'Yes. Anyway, to continue. He's reasonably familiar with prison life, though the police would feel he should be even more so if he'd always got his just deserts.

'On this last occasion he broke into the flat of a man named Milos Bilak and stole six thousand pounds cash. Mr

Bilak was away at the time and, having neutralised various security devices, Eddie had time to make himself a cup of coffee and give the place a thorough search. When he left, the flat was as neat and tidy as when he arrived. Nothing was out of place save for the six thousand pounds he had transferred into the capacious pockets of his burglar's outfit.' She paused. 'But even the Eddie Rudings of this life can't guard against outrageous fortune. As he made his descent to the ground via a drainpipe and fire escape, he virtually dropped into the embrace of a young PC who made the easiest arrest that's ever likely to come his way.'

'So what was his defence?'

'A very simple one. That he burgled Bilak's flat at the behest of the Security Service. He was sent there to find a code book Bilak was supposed to have.'

'Did he find it?'

Rosa shook her head. 'The six thousand pounds was, as you might say, a personal bonus, but not for long. It not only incriminated him, but diminished the credibility of his defence, as the prosecution was quick to point out.'

'Did you try and substantiate what he'd told you?'

'Of course, but I got nowhere. MI5 had no intention of stepping forward to support him. I met with firmly closed doors and telephone calls that usually left me talking to myself.'

'I presume he gave you the name of the person in MI5 who put him up to it?'

'It was somebody called Colin Kirby, an ex-member of the Rhodesian Police when that force existed. He was not only unhelpful, but ungracious with it.'

'Did you meet him?'

'No. We only spoke on the phone. I told Ruding to let me know if he spotted him in court. But it was obvious he wasn't going to show his face at the trial.'

'But the fact that he existed goes some way to show that Ruding was telling the truth,' Peter observed.

Rosa sighed. 'Not necessarily. I don't doubt that at

some point in his criminal career, Eddie Ruding had crossed Kirby's path – not that Kirby admitted any such thing – but that didn't help his defence. As it was, his word stood alone like a guttering candle that was finally snuffed out. The judge saw to that. He told the jury how easy it was for an accused man to advance a fanciful defence that sought to turn a straightforward burglary into a romantic spy drama. He pointed out that no mysterious code books had been found in Ruding's possession, but that six thousand pounds in cash had been; money which came from the flat he had just burgled.' Rosa let out another sigh. 'I'm afraid Eddie Ruding sank himself by his opportunism.'

'One can see that he would have regarded it as a wasted opportunity to leave the money behind,' Peter remarked. 'But nothing yet explains what he's doing in Amsterdam a few weeks after he received a sentence of five years.'

'Or why my presence appears to have upset somebody's plans.'

Peter frowned. 'Did you have a chance to look at the faces of his two companions?'

'Not properly. As far as I know I'd never seen either of them before.'

'I wondered if they might have been in court during Ruding's trial?'

Rosa gave a shrug. 'I've no idea.'

'One was dark and swarthy, the other tough and blond. The blond one gave the impression of being a bodyguard. I suspect he carried a gun amongst his padding.'

'What about the cyclist?' Rosa asked. 'Would you recognise him again?'

'He had the sort of face you see at a football punch-up when the fans are getting to know each other.' He gave Rosa a long steady look before speaking again. 'Would you like to cut our visit short and go home today?' he asked.

'No,' Rosa said with a vigorous shake of her head.

'It's possible that Ruding and his friends may have something further in store.'

16

'I doubt it. I think that was probably a one-off attempt to put me out of action. It was an instant response to what they regarded as a threatening situation. If it had succeeded, they were rid of me in circumstances pointing to an accident and the truth would be unlikely ever to emerge. But now, for all they know, we've been in touch with the police. I suspect that Eddie Ruding and his friends have already skipped the city. Or, at least, are lying very low.'

Peter pursed his lips. 'You're sure you want to stay?'

'Quite sure. I know I was worried when I saw Ruding at the café yesterday, but the situation has developed since then. A bit like a boil that's burst.'

'Do you still intend to do some investigating when you get back to London?'

'Certainly I do.'

'I doubt whether you'll find MI5 any more co-operative than they were before.'

'I shall start with Detective Sergeant Crisp. He was the divisional officer in charge of the case and a reasonable sort of person.' She pushed back her chair and got up. Moving round behind Peter's chair she bent forward and kissed him on the cheek. 'I like your new aftershave . . .'

Before she could say anything further, he had pulled her head down and put his lips against hers. Rosa surrendered to his embrace.

'Shall we go to the van Gogh museum after all today?' he said, when they eventually drew apart. 'I have a feeling you're fitter than I expected.'

Rosa smiled. 'I can't think we'll run into Eddie Ruding and his friends there. Not for them all those sunflowers and blue irises.'

Chapter Three

'Ah, you're back!'

Stephanie, Snaith and Epton's indispensable telephonist-cum-receptionist, had a unique ability to bring somebody down to earth. It was with these words delivered dispassionately that she greeted Rosa's return to the office early on Tuesday afternoon.

'Mr Snaith has the tax inspector with him,' she went on, 'and Ben has had to take work to Mr Radford as he's hurt his back and can't get into the office and the phone has hardly stopped ringing.' She paused. 'Did you have a nice time?'

Stephanie knew more about the office than anyone. Not only about its workload, but about the hitches and hiccups in the lives of its staff. She and Rosa enjoyed a special rapport and Rosa would have trusted her with her innermost secrets.

Rosa put down her bag (she had come straight from the airport) and decided to start at the top of Stephanie's itemised list of information.

'What on earth is the tax man doing here?' she asked, glancing at Robin's door.

'Something to do with the firm's claim in respect of office redecoration. But I don't think you need worry, I've heard them laughing.'

'And you say Ben's had to take work to Mr Radford's home. How long is he going to be on the sick list?'

Ben was the firm's genial outdoor clerk, who would turn his hand to anything. Rosa had rescued him from a life of petty crime and had never had reason to regret offering him employment. He and Stephanie enjoyed the sort of relationship that develops between a newly arrived puppy and the household's well-established cat. As for Mr Radford, he was a retired bookkeeper who came in two afternoons a week to look after that side of the firm's work.

He had a heavily lined face, piercing eyes and teeth that clicked like castanets, though he seemed totally unaware of the distracting sounds that accompanied every utterance.

'He should be back next week,' Stephanie said. 'He did it gardening, the old fool!'

Mr Radford had once rested a hand on Stephanie's knee and been out of favour ever since, though Stephanie was quite capable of dealing with a dozen Mr Radfords at one and the same time.

'So you enjoyed yourself in Amsterdam?' she went on.

'Very much.'

'And Peter, too?'

'Likewise.'

Rosa stooped to pick up her bag before going to her room to see how high was the pile of work that awaited her attention.

'Do you want to take calls,' Stephanie enquired, 'or shall I make excuses?'

'I'd sooner not be disturbed, Steph, unless it's something urgent. I have a number of phone calls of my own to make.' Stephanie gave her a quick look, but said nothing. 'Here's a small present from the Duty Free,' Rosa added, handing her a gift-wrapped bottle of perfume. 'It's from me and Peter. It's his thank-you for all the phone calls you fielded while he was in Hong Kong. He says you're the most efficient telephonist in the world.'

'Ask him to let me have that in writing. And thank you both very much.'

Rosa moved toward her room, then paused. 'Has there been anything in the papers about Eddie Ruding while I've been away?' she asked.

'Not that I've seen. If there had been anything, I'm sure Ben would have spotted it.'

Rosa nodded. Ben had a sharp nose for newspaper items about the firm's clients and seldom missed anything.

'I'll ask him when he gets back if you like,' Stephanie went on.

'Don't bother. It was just that I saw his double in Amsterdam and wondered if he'd made a prison break.'

'Why not call the officer in charge? It was Detective Sergeant Crisp, if I recall.'

'Maybe I'll do that,' Rosa remarked in what was meant to be a casual tone, not that it deceived Stephanie.

She spent the next half-hour glancing through the papers in her in-tray and allotting them priority. After this she felt better, for, at least, she now knew the worst, though there didn't appear to be anything of particular urgency awaiting attention. Except, of course, that every client regarded his case as requiring instant attention and it was usually those who created the biggest fuss who received it. 'Blessed are the meek for they shall inherit the earth' didn't apply in solicitors' offices.

She lifted her telephone and asked Stephanie to get Detective Sergeant Crisp. A moment later the connection was made.

'Good afternoon, Miss Epton,' Crisp said in the wary tone often adopted by police officers when taking calls from defence solicitors. 'What can I do for you?'

'I was wondering if you happened to have any information about Eddie Ruding?'

There appeared to be a considerable pause before he replied.

'No, none,' he said, at length. 'Anyway, what sort of information?'

'I thought you might have had occasion to visit him in prison.'

'No, I haven't. As far as I'm concerned, he's just a criminal statistic.'

'Do you know which prison he's in?'

'No. In fact I no longer have his docket here. CI sent for it shortly after his trial and it's not been returned. Not that I'm bothered. It's one less file to collect dust.'

'You've no idea why CI wanted it?'

'None at all, Miss Epton. I've learnt never to question

20

the motives of my superiors; in particular, what goes on in the upper reaches of the Yard.' He paused again before adding, 'In the same way I'm not asking you why you're suddenly interested in Ruding. I take it you're not thinking of lodging a late appeal against conviction?'

'I have no instructions to that effect.'

'Good.'

For a while after she had rung off, Rosa sat staring in thought across her office. Sergeant Crisp may have been deliberately stalling, but she didn't think so. If he had been, he would have been unlikely to have disclosed that he had been required to send the Ruding case papers to headquarters. He purported not to know why and this could be the truth. Meanwhile, Rosa was left wondering what might have been the reason.

If the police were unable to help her, maybe MI5 could. She would phone Kirby. After all, she might learn something from the nature of the brush-off she received. Getting through to him, however, required both patience and determination. Members of the Security Service appeared to be shielded by ladies made of steel who had considerable experience in seeing off importunate callers.

It was from Eddie Ruding himself that Rosa had originally received a telephone number for contacting Kirby. The first time she used it, he had clearly been extremely displeased. Nevertheless she had got through to him and this seemed to indicate that he and Ruding were known to each other, not that Kirby ever admitted it in so many words. She was prepared to believe, however, that Ruding had, for his own purposes, moved dates and places to involve Kirby in the burglary at Bilak's flat. It was common enough practice amongst criminals, particularly in the establishment of an alibi. No need to invent facts, just move them to a more convenient date.

Rosa dialled his number and after a number of clicks and untoward noises found herself addressing one of the ladies of steel.

21

'I'd like to speak to Mr Colin Kirby, please,' she said.
'And your name?'
'Rosa Epton. I'm a solicitor.'
'I don't think you're through to the right extension,' the voice said, as if responding to the opening move in a game of chess.
'It's the extension on which I spoke to him previously.'
'Hold on.'
The line appeared to go dead and Rosa was just thinking she had already been checkmated, when Kirby's clipped, nasal tones broke in on her thoughts.
'You wish to speak to me, Miss Epton?' He sounded no more friendly than on previous occasions.
'Yes, about Eddie Ruding.'
'What about him?'
'As far as you know is he still in prison?'
'What an extraordinary question to ask me! I suggest you address it to the Home Office Prison Department.'
There was a pause and Rosa waited, hoping that his curiosity would get the better of him. She was rewarded, for a few moments later he said, 'Anyway, what makes you think he mayn't still be in prison?'
'I never suggested that he wasn't.'
'Your question implied it. I thought you were going to tell me that he'd been in touch with you.'
'No,' Rosa said, having already decided not to mention events in Amsterdam.
'Well, that's that then. As far as I'm concerned, Ruding was completely out of order in trying to involve me in his criminal activities. It does happen from time to time that criminals take our name in vain in an attempt to bamboozle a jury. I would hope that you'd discourage any of your clients from making that sort of mischief. It doesn't do anyone any good and one hopes that their lawyers won't abet them.'
On this uncompromising note, their conversation ended. The fact that Kirby came on the line at all was, Rosa felt, of some significance, though nothing had been said which

answered any of the questions bubbling in her mind.

She decided that her next call should be to Eddie's mother who lived on a council estate south of the river. They had spoken on the phone pending her son's trial, but had not met. Rosa had expected her to turn up at court, but Eddie said he had told her to stay away.

Rosa's impression had been of a hard-working woman in her sixties who doted on her erring son and would do or say anything to help him.

As she dialled the number, she wondered what she would say if Eddie himself answered the telephone. In the event, she obtained no reply either then or later.

When they met for dinner that evening, she and Peter discussed the latest developments and decided there was nothing further to be done, either immediately or maybe ever. It would remain one of those mysteries that are never satisfactorily resolved. Eddie Ruding would be a story without an ending.

And so it might have been, had fate not decided to lend a further hand.

Chapter Four

It was about two weeks later and Rosa had spent the morning conferring with a client who was charged with fraud on a bank. Rosa normally had little sympathy with banks, which often seemed to aid and abet fraud on their corporate selves by a mixture of cupidity and negligence. In this instance, however, she was even more exasperated by the attitude of her client, which was one of pious self-pity. The bank, he complained, had no right to have allowed him to defraud it so easily. It was they who should be standing in the dock, not himself. Rosa gathered that by 'they' he meant the chairman, the executive directors and the local manager.

By the time the client had departed and she had tidied her desk it was nearly two o'clock and she decided to go out for half an hour. She would have a cup of coffee at the Italian café round the corner and might even be tempted to have a toasted cheese sandwich.

Stephanie was at her post in reception, waiting to be relieved by Ben who usually manned the switchboard when she went out. She and Rosa were exchanging views on a new shoe shop in the vicinity when the outer door flew open to admit Ben.

He invariably spent his lunch break trying to pick winners from the afternoon race card and so always returned to the office with a mauled copy of the midday paper.

His face lit up on seeing Rosa and she could tell that he was bursting with news of some sort.

Thrusting the newspaper at her, he said excitedly, 'There's something about your client, Ruding, in the paper, Miss E. He had a fall trying to escape from prison and broke his neck. He was found lying at the foot of the prison wall with a length of rope near by.'

He handed the newspaper to Rosa who read:

'Prisoner Killed in Escape Bid.' Beneath this sub-headline, the piece ran:

A prisoner of the name of Edward Ruding was found dead at the foot of an outside wall at Wandsworth Prison around six o'clock this morning. It appeared that the rope he was using to lower himself had broken and he had fallen to the ground. The prison referred all enquiries to the Home Office where an official declined to make any statement at this stage. It is understood that an investigation is already under way. A man named Edward Ruding was sentenced to five years' imprisonment for burglary at the Old Bailey earlier this year.

'Sounds like your client all right, Miss E,' Ben went on when he saw that she had finished reading the piece.

Apart from her partner, Robin Snaith, Rosa had not told anyone in the office of what had happened in Amsterdam. Stephanie might have gleaned something from her key position on the switchboard, but Ben was wholly unaware of events in Holland. Thanking him, she handed him back his paper.

'He must have had an accomplice waiting to pick him up in a car, but I don't suppose he hung around for long,' Ben remarked with a certain relish. 'Must have been a bit of a shock for the bloke.'

Half an hour later, when Rosa returned to the office from the café, she went to see if Robin was back from his morning in court.

While her coffee had been slowly cooling, she had had time to think about what had happened. Assuming it was Eddie Ruding who was dead, it just didn't make sense. At least, not that he had died while escaping from prison.

Robin greeted her with a smile and waved her to a chair. He could always tell from Rosa's expression when something was troubling her.

'Take a seat and unburden yourself,' he said amiably.

'Is that how I look?'

'Near enough.'

'It's about Ruding once more.'

'I thought it might be.'

'Did Ben show you his paper?'

'You didn't expect him not to spread the tidings, did you?'

'So what do you think?'

'Obviously MI5 have been up to their games. They're trained to move in mysterious ways their wonders to perform. Save that in their case, the wonders are often on the squalid side and of dubious value.'

'But it doesn't make sense that Ruding was first released from prison, then finds himself back inside and finally breaks his neck trying to escape.'

'It doesn't make any sense at all, but that's because we don't know the full story. When that emerges, if it

25

ever does, we'll probably have a very different picture.' He gave Rosa a wry smile. 'I know you'll find it a maddening prospect, but there's nothing you can do except sit back and wait. It's possible the police will want to interview you, but that's by no means certain. It'll depend on which direction their enquiries take.'

'You don't think I should tell them that I saw him in Amsterdam?'

'No,' Robin said after a thoughtful pause. 'Not yet, anyway. More details are bound to filter out in the next few days, so I'd recommend a wait-and-see policy.'

'If you're right about MI5's involvement, we're unlikely to get a true picture.'

'Let's wait, anyway. You've already spoken to Sergeant Crisp and Kirby since you got back and neither of them gave you any change. Phoning the prison governor would be equally unproductive. You need status before you start demanding answers to questions. In the affair of Edward Ruding, his life and death, Snaith and Epton lack professional status. We're nothing more than interested by-standers.'

It was a little speech that Robin felt compelled to deliver to his junior partner from time to time when she was straining at the leash to involve herself in what he referred to as extra-curricular activities.

As soon as she was dressed the next morning, Rosa went out to the local newsagent and bought a selection of morning papers. She took them home and laid them out on the kitchen table beside a cup of Earl Grey tea which constituted her breakfast most days.

All the papers carried an account of Eddie Ruding's death, though in most of them it had the texture of candy floss. A lurid headline and very little substance. In one, however, the *Morning Gazette*, the reporter had obviously felt that there was a story worth digging out beneath the bare facts.

Under the headline, 'Mystery Surrounds Prisoner's Death

26

Fall', there appeared the following by the paper's correspondent, Clive Fox:

Considerable mystery surrounds the death of Edward Ruding, the prisoner whose body was found yesterday morning at the foot of Wandsworth Prison wall. It is understood that a post mortem has revealed he died of a broken neck. But was this as a result of his fall and, if not, how did he break his neck? As yet these questions remain unanswered and the prison authorities are refusing to say anything. The police are being equally unforthcoming. When I spoke to a prison officer as he came off duty, he told me they had been instructed not to talk about the incident to outsiders. For obvious reasons he didn't wish to be identified, but added that there were rumours that Ruding had been killed by a waiting accomplice. It seems clear there must have been an accomplice, but he's vanished into thin air.

The inference is that Ruding was assisted in his escape, only then to be murdered. In fact that his escape was a trap.

The prison officer to whom I spoke didn't personally know Ruding. He said that with a prison population the size of Wandsworth's and a constant turnover of inmates, you only got to know the long-term residents and those who made a nuisance of themselves.

At his Old Bailey trial where he was convicted of burglary at a flat leased by a Czech business man, Ruding's defence was that he was put up to it by MI5, for whom he had previously worked on a freelance basis. A spokesman for the Security Service said it was a ludicrous and preposterous suggestion.

So the mystery of Ruding's death is wrapped in a further mystery.

Rosa put down the paper and reached for her cup of now tepid tea. She was surprised that Clive Fox had written

27

his piece without approaching her. Though slightly niggled about this, she was also glad that he hadn't. She was wondering how much she would have told him, when her phone rang.

'Is that Rosa Epton?' a brisk male voice enquired.

'Yes.'

'I'm Clive Fox of the *Morning Gazette*. I believe you were Eddie Ruding's solicitor?'

'That's correct. And before you go any further, Mr Fox, let me say that I've just read your piece in today's paper.'

'You have? Then, you'll know why I'm calling. I'm afraid it was a bit of a rush job, but in journalism time waits for no man. As a matter of fact I did try and contact you yesterday, but your switchboard girl wasn't very helpful. One could say downright uncooperative. Said she had orders not to disturb you, even though I told her it was urgent.'

Rosa smiled to herself. Clive Fox had clearly been no match for Stephanie, who had a particular dislike of people she regarded as pushy. Nevertheless, it was unlike Steph not to have mentioned his call. Then she remembered that their indispensable Girl Friday had left the office early to go to the dentist.

'Tell me,' Fox now went on in the same forceful tone, 'what did you think of my piece? Don't you agree there's something fishy about Ruding's death? I'd like to have your views on him. Why don't we meet and have a talk? I can come along to your office this morning.'

'I'm afraid I shall be tied up all day,' Rosa said quickly. She had already decided that she didn't wish to make an ally of Clive Fox.

'Don't you want the truth to come out?' he asked in a faintly hectoring tone.

'It's just that I don't feel I have anything useful to contribute.'

'Let me be the judge of that.'

'I've really nothing further to say.'

28

'Well, nobody's going to stop me digging away. I'm certain there's a good story waiting to be told and the public are entitled to have it. If you change your mind, let me know.'

'I will.'

'By the way, does the name Colin Kirby ring any bells?'

'Yes.'

'You know him?'

'I know of him.'

'Was he a friend of Ruding's?'

'I think they were acquainted.'

'I'm told that at Ruding's trial an MI5 officer's name was mentioned. Except that it wasn't mentioned, it was written on a piece of paper to preserve his anonymity. The fact I regard that as typical of the double standards practised in our so-called open courts is neither here nor there, but was Kirby the name of the officer in question?'

'No comment.'

'Which means that it was.'

'Which means no comment.'

'Why won't you answer a perfectly straightforward question?'

'Because in view of the judge's order, I'd be in contempt of court. I don't think this conversation is going to get us any further.'

'And yet you were sufficiently interested to have read my piece in the *Gazette* at this relatively early hour of the day. Would I be right in thinking you went out specially to buy the paper?' He paused, and when Rosa didn't reply went on, 'All right, don't answer that if you don't want to, though I can't help thinking that our paths will cross again.'

He rang off, leaving Rosa feeling as if she had been run over by another tram. She may have felt a slight resentment that he had not been in touch before writing his piece, but he had now rectified the omission. Rosa decided that Stephanie had coped with him better than she had.

She reached her front door, paused and turned back. She

29

would try and reach Peter on the phone and tell him what had happened. He had been out of London the previous day and was due home only at midnight.

'Peter, it's me,' she said when a somewhat sleepy voice answered.

'What time is it?'

'Eight forty-five.'

'Why don't you come round for breakfast?'

'Stop asking questions and listen.'

When she had finished telling him of Eddie Ruding's death and of Clive Fox's call, he said, 'Hmm.'

'Didn't you read of Eddie's death in last night's evening paper?' she asked a trifle querulously.

'No. As soon as I got on the plane I fell asleep. I woke up only when we landed and fell asleep again on the ride into London.'

'Sounds as if you had an exhausting day.'

'My client was more than usually demanding.'

'Another millionaire, I suppose?'

'I hope so. Anyway, give me time to think. I'll have a shower and call you in the office. It seems the plot is thickening.'

Peter's interest in her cases was always zestful and he was apt to brush aside any reminder of their relative earnings in the law.

'Money's not everything,' he would say.

'It is when you have a mortgage to pay,' she invariably replied.

She had scarcely reached the office when Stephanie announced that Peter was on the line.

'I've been thinking,' he said.

'And?'

'Put everything on a back burner until we have dinner this evening.'

'That all?'

'Yes.'

Rosa reflected that it was all very well telling her to put

everything on a back burner, but the matter wasn't entirely in her hands.

And so it proved to be.

From time to time something went awry with the office switchboard and callers would find themselves speaking directly to an extension without Stephanie's intervention.

'It's Mrs Ruding,' a voice said when Rosa picked up her phone that afternoon. 'Mrs Charlotte Ruding,' the voice added in case Rosa might know more than one. 'You defended my Eddie at the Old Bailey.'

'I was very sorry to read about his death,' Rosa broke in.

'That's what I'm phoning you about. I'd like to come and see you. Will this afternoon be convenient?'

Rosa glanced at her watch. It was three thirty. 'I'll be in my office until around six,' she said.

'I'll come straightaway.'

'I did try and call you yesterday as soon as I read about Eddie's death,' Rosa said, 'but you weren't at home.'

'I've moved, and what the papers say is all lies.'

On this uncompromising note she rang off. It was about an hour later that Stephanie buzzed Rosa and said, 'I have Mrs Ruding in reception. She says you're expecting her.'

'Yes, I am. Could you ask Ben to bring her to my room?'

A few seconds later there was a knock on the door and Ben flung it open with the air of a bit-part actor making the most of a small role.

'Mrs Charlotte Ruding,' he announced, standing aside.

Rosa's first impression was of someone as wide as she was tall. Mrs Ruding was wearing a dress with a bold floral pattern which did nothing to diminish her size. Her hair was a frizzy red which was definitely not one of nature's colours.

'Come in, Mrs Ruding,' Rosa said, extending a hand in greeting.

Her visitor glanced nervously about her, before perching herself on the edge of an upright chair.

'When did you move?' Rosa asked, in an attempt to break the ice.

'Soon after Eddie's trial. They said it would be better.'

'They?'

'They said they was Eddie's friends, but they wasn't.' She compressed her lips in a forbidding line as she continued to take in her surroundings like a cat weighing up a strange room. Then fixing her gaze on Rosa, she said, 'I don't rightly know where to begin.'

'Did you visit Eddie in prison after his trial?' Rosa prompted.

'Once in the Scrubs and then 'e was moved.'

'Did you go and see him in Wandsworth?'

She shook her head. 'I didn't even know 'e was there. If 'e ever was.'

Rosa drew a deep breath. 'Do you know anything about your son getting out of prison?'

'I 'ad this message saying 'e was all right and I didn't know what it meant. Then a day or two later Eddie phoned me and said I wasn't to worry and 'e'd see me sooner than I expected. I asked 'im where 'e was and 'e said 'e was with friends.'

'Was that before or after you'd moved?'

'It was the next day this man came to see me and said Eddie wanted me to move, otherwise I might be bothered by newspapers. I told 'im not to be ridiculous and that I wasn't going to move just like that. So he picks up the phone and dials a number and the next thing I 'ear is Eddie's voice and 'e asks me to do as the man says for 'is sake. 'E said it was a friend's flat I was to go and stay in, just temporary like.'

'Where is the flat?'

'Out 'Ounslow way.'

She managed to make the Borough of Hounslow sound as if it were on the further face of the moon.

'When did you last hear from Eddie?'

'About a week ago. 'E said 'e'd been away but 'oped

to see me soon and everything was fine. I asked 'im where 'e was, but 'e just said 'e was OK. A few days later 'e sent me some money in an envelope.'

'Did you notice where it had been posted?'

'Didn't think to look until after I'd thrown it away.'

'When did you first learn about Eddie's death?'

'Not till I sees it in the paper,' she said and wiped away a solitary tear.

'Has anyone phoned you?'

'Nobody. That's why I decided to come and see you. I'm sure my Eddie never died the way they says. 'E was murdered.'

'Who do you think might have murdered him?' Rosa asked.

Mrs Ruding pursed her lips and stared stonily at the carpet.

'Eddie was the best son any mother could 'ave 'ad,' she said in a tone that prepared Rosa for a seamless blend of fact and fiction about her dead son. "E 'ad 'is difficult times, but what boy doesn't? But 'e always used to say, "You come first, Mum," and 'e meant it. Mind you, I didn't always like the company 'e kept. 'E could be led astray. 'E got that from his father. Eddie was only fourteen when my husband walked out on us. I should never 'ave married a foreigner. 'E was Dutch, you see. Not set eyes on 'im since.' She stared into the distance as if conjuring up her husband's face.

Rosa took the opportunity to try and bring her narrative up to date.

'I don't doubt that Eddie was a good son to you, Mrs Ruding, but the fact remains he was in trouble with the law on a number of occasions.'

'Like I said, 'e could be easily led. 'E was too good-natured.'

Rosa's own impression had been of an artful, streetwise criminal who was capable of turning on charm of a sort if he thought it might serve a purpose.

'What do you know about this last offence that led him to prison?'

''E was put up to it by others.'

'What others?'

'If you ask me, it was Tam Grigg's lot.'

'Who's Tam Grigg?' Rosa asked, as she wondered where their conversation was going to end.

'The Griggs used to live next to us in Bermondsey. A real bad lot, they was. When they moved away, I thought good riddance. Then I found out my Eddie was still seeing Tam. 'E's a year or two older than Eddie and twice 'is size. Used to bash Eddie when they was kids . . .'

'And yet they remained friends.'

'Eddie was under Tam's influence.'

'Do you know where Tam is now?'

'I know where 'e ought to be. Behind bars.'

Rosa was thoughtful for a while. 'What exactly is it you want me to do, Mrs Ruding?'

'Find out for sure who killed my Eddie.'

'That's a job for the police.'

'The police!' Mrs Ruding echoed scornfully. 'The police don't care. As far as they're concerned, Eddie's no loss to anyone. But that's where they're wrong because 'e's a loss to 'is mother and I want you to find out the truth.'

'You're quite convinced he didn't die breaking out of prison?'

Rosa received a withering look. 'Course 'e didn't.'

'How can you be so positive?'

'I'll tell you 'ow. 'E couldn't stand 'ights. 'E'd never 'ave climbed a prison wall. 'E used to get giddy looking out of a first-floor window.'

'That could be the reason he fell. He was overcome by giddiness.'

'But 'e wasn't in prison at the time.'

That was also Rosa's view, but she wanted to test everything Mrs Ruding told her as far as she could.

'Did the police ever come to your house looking for him?'

'When do you mean?'

'Between his trial and his death?'

'No, never.'

'There was never any hint that he'd escaped from prison?'

'From the police, you mean?'

Rosa nodded.

'Never set eyes on that Sergeant Crisp after Eddie went down,' Mrs Ruding said contemptuously. ''E came to the 'ouse after Eddie's arrest, but I wasn't going to give 'im anything. Not even a cup of tea without milk and sugar.'

Mrs Ruding and Rosa exchanged thoughtful stares for several seconds.

'So who do you think could have killed your son?' Rosa asked, breaking the silence.

'Tam Grigg, like I've said.'

'For what motive?'

She gave a dismissive shrug. 'Tam wouldn't need a motive. Maybe my Eddie 'ad served 'is purpose and 'ad to be got rid of.'

'A gang killing, you mean?'

'Tam knows all about them.'

Rosa sighed. 'I really don't see how I can help you, Mrs Ruding. It's not my line of work and I don't have the resources.'

Mrs Ruding gave her a reproachful look. 'Eddie thought 'ighly of you and told me to come to you if anything 'appened.' She opened her handbag. ''Ere's five 'undred pounds. There's more if you want it.'

Rosa shook her head. 'I don't want any money now. Give me time to think and I'll get in touch with you tomorrow and let you know my decision.'

Mrs Ruding put the money back into her handbag and closed it with a pronounced snap. She was halfway to the door when Rosa spoke again.

'Did Eddie have any family or friends in Amsterdam?'

'Only Vincent – and 'is father if 'e's still alive.'

'Who's Vincent?'

'My eldest boy,' Mrs Ruding said in a grudging tone.
'Eddie's brother?'

'Yes. When my 'usband walked out, Vincent was seven-teen and went with 'is father. 'E's lived in 'Olland ever since, but I've not seen 'im.' She spoke as if the words had a bitter taste.

'Did Eddie keep in touch with his brother?'

''E could 'ave done,' she said dismissively.

It was clear to Rosa that the two brothers had maintained contact, if without the blessing of their formidable mother. Eddie had never mentioned his brother to Rosa, but there was no particular reason why he should have done so. She now wondered, however, if one of the men with him in the café had been Vincent? There was no obvious significance in Mrs Ruding having cut her elder son out of her life and having focused all her affection on his younger brother.

'Do I have your telephone number?' Rosa enquired as she got up to escort Mrs Ruding from the room.

'I'll ring you. Don't like giving my number around these days. I don't mean I don't trust you. I do. Well, anyway Eddie did. But if you're not going to 'elp, you don't need it.' She walked down the corridor and reached reception with Rosa just behind her. 'You got Eddie off the first time 'e came to you,' she said as she opened the main door. 'I remember 'e didn't want a woman brief. Thought you might be a pushover for the police, but I told 'im that a woman can be as tough as a man. With me as 'is mum, 'e shouldn't 'ave needed reminding, should 'e?'

Then with a quick nod of her red, frizzy head, she departed.

'So that's Eddie Ruding's mother,' Stephanie observed as Rosa turned to go back to her room.

'A cockney matriarch. They can fight like tigresses.'

'Better to have as mothers than as mothers-in-law.'

Rosa laughed. 'You have a point there, Steph. Per-haps that's why her Eddie doesn't appear to have had a girlfriend.'

36

'What are you minded to do now?' Peter asked as he and Rosa sat over their pre-dinner drinks in the small French restaurant where they often ate. Though it was expensive, it was not yet outrageously so and Jean-Paul picked his customers with care, flatly refusing to accept bookings from those he didn't like the look or sound of.

'I don't see what I can do,' Rosa said. 'I'm not a private eye. As I told Mrs Ruding, I don't have the resources to undertake investigations that properly belong to the police.'

'You have me, the reincarnation of Charlie Chan.'

Rosa smiled. 'So what do you suggest, Charlie?'

'I agree there's a limit to what you can do, even with my help. But don't forget you have a personal stake in the matter. Remember what happened in Amsterdam.'

'Amsterdam seems an aeon ago.'

'Eighteen days to be exact. Eighteen days since an attempt was made on your life. By the way, did you tell Mrs Ruding about that?'

Rosa shook her head. 'I decided against.'

'Probably wise. I can't help wondering if Eddie's mother is as straightforward as she made herself out to be.'

'I think most of what she told me was probably the truth. But was it the whole truth? If I do decide to accept her instructions, it'll mean finding out something about Vincent and also trying to discover whether Tam Grigg could have had anything to do with Eddie's death. Though heaven knows how I set about that.'

'I can help on both scores. I can nip over to Amsterdam for the day and try and run Vincent to earth. And I have contacts who may know something of Grigg.'

Peter's contacts were innumerable and seemed to embrace the whole spectrum of society.

In a thoughtful voice Rosa said, 'I think that before I decide what to do, I should await the inquest on Eddie. I need to know the pathologist's findings. If he did die as a result of falling off the wall, it's an end of the matter.'

'Or the start of a new chapter,' Peter remarked. He picked up the menu that had been left on their table. 'But first things first, let's decide what we're going to eat.'

Chapter 5

Earlier that day, four men had gathered round a table at the Home Office.

Two were from that department, an under-secretary with responsibilities for prisons and a member of the Secretary of State's private office. The other two were a deputy assistant commissioner from Scotland Yard and a senior administrator from MI5.

'Why did he have to go and get himself killed?' the senior of the two Home Office men asked crossly.

'I know,' said his colleague with the air of urbanity that seldom deserted him. 'It was a mark of extreme ingratitude.'

The man from the Prison Department gave him a frosty look. 'Well, it's left us in an extremely embarrassing situation and one that's potentially explosive as far as the Home Secretary is concerned. He's not at all happy with what's happened.'

'Damage limitation is obviously the name of the game,' said the man from MI5. 'Though that's easier said than done.'

The three men turned their gaze on the Deputy Assistant Commissioner, who had not yet spoken.

'This is where you come in,' said the senior Home Office man. 'It's vital you hand-pick the right officer to conduct the enquiry. It'll need very delicate handling.'

The DAC smiled. He knew he was in a less vulnerable position than the others. They were all tainted by what had happened, whereas he was a new arrival on the scene.

'I take it nobody's suggesting the police should engage in a cover-up?' he said.

'Who said anything about cover-ups?' the man from the Prison Department asked sharply. 'There's all the difference between a carefully handled enquiry and a cover-up.'

'That's all right then,' the DAC said with a small, complacent smile his companions could have done without. 'What's the reaction of the prison governor? Presumably he's aware that the dead man wasn't one of his inmates?'

'Of course.'

'I imagine', said the man from the Home Secretary's private office, 'he finds it a joke in exceedingly poor taste.'

'It was a thoroughly mischief-making thing to do,' said his colleague in a reproving tone. 'If somebody wanted to kill Ruding, as somebody obviously did, he could have accomplished it in a hundred and one other ways.'

'Obviously a troublemaker,' observed the other Home Office man.

'I just wish we'd never been drawn into the whole sordid deal.' He glared at the man from MI5. 'I hope your chap, Kirby, is feeling suitably chastened.'

'I don't see that the blame can be laid at his door,' MI5 replied robustly. 'He did no more than his duty in making his recommendation. It was a Home Office decision to release Ruding.'

'Only because of your urgent representations,' said prison department. He let out a heavy sigh and went on, 'I suppose these things are bound to happen when people with criminal records are recruited by your service for felonious exploits. It's happened before. Personally, I'd ban the practice.'

'Who would MI5 then get to do their burglaries?' his colleague enquired sardonically.

The DAC decided it was time to intervene in the bickering. 'Are there any theories as to who may have killed Ruding? I'd like to give my officer something to work on.'

'I've spoken to Kirby about that,' said MI5, 'but I'm afraid he isn't of much help. He says that Ruding was a professional burglar of considerable skill. When he briefed him for the Bilak job, he didn't go further than satisfying himself he was capable of doing it.'

'Which he wasn't, in the event,' prison department remarked sourly.

'I think it's fair to say that Ruding's arrest was pure bad luck. None of us can guard against that.'

'Dare one enquire', asked private office, 'how Kirby came to know someone with such tip-top credentials in the burglary business?'

MI5 frowned. It was not really a permissible question, though in the circumstances he saw no harm in answering it.

'Kirby met him in prison. I don't mean that Kirby was serving a sentence, but he went there to interview someone who had information we were interested in. While there, he met the man's cellmate who was Ruding. The man Kirby was visiting described him as the best cat burglar left in the business. Kirby kept this in mind, and when the right opportunity came along decided to use him.'

'Fascinating,' murmured private office in an aside.

'Wouldn't it have been better if Ruding had been persuaded to plead guilty at his trial?' the DAC asked. 'He could still have been quietly released afterwards and it would have prevented his publicly involving the Security Service.'

'I agree,' said MI5. 'Between ourselves I don't think Kirby handled that aspect very well. Trouble was that once the die was cast, there was no going back. And don't forget that Ruding himself didn't stick to the rules. He helped himself to a large sum of cash which was certainly not part of his assignment. It placed Kirby in a very awkward position.'

Private office assumed an even more sardonic expression. If any of this ever got out, the press would have a field day and the unfortunate Home Secretary would find himself facing music of Wagnerian dimensions when he stood up to answer questions in Parliament. Indeed, an accompaniment of the final scene of *Götterdämmerung* might not be inappropriate, with its fire, floods and funeral pyres.

'Well, it looks as if my officer will have to start from scratch,' the DAC observed, glancing round the table. 'Though I have the impression that not too many tears will be shed if the investigation comes to nought.'

Nobody made any comment and shortly thereafter the meeting broke up.

Chapter 6

Detective Chief Inspector Richard Cain was a calm, unflappable officer who preferred to keep a low profile at work. It was this virtue, amongst others, which had persuaded the DAC that he was the right officer to investigate Eddie Ruding's death. The DAC's first thought had been to appoint a detective superintendent, even a chief superintendent, to conduct the enquiry, but then he decided that a competent officer of less exalted rank might be a better choice.

Cain left the DAC's office somewhat nonplussed by the instructions he had been given. He enjoyed his job, however, and this was just another assignment, albeit one with ill-defined guidelines.

Find out who killed Eddie Ruding without causing an atomic explosion was the gist of what he had been told. To which the DAC had added, 'And good luck.'

By the time Cain reached his own office, he had decided that his starting point would be a visit to the pathologist who had conducted a post mortem examination on Ruding.

Twenty minutes later he was on his way out of the building.

Busy forensic pathologists spend their time hanging about

courts waiting to give evidence and dashing from one mortuary to the next where bodies uncomplainingly await their arrival.

Dr Felling had just completed an autopsy when Cain arrived.

'Hello, Chief Inspector. I got your message and you've come at just the right moment. I don't think we've met before, have we?'

'Yes, sir. Several years ago when I was a detective sergeant at Richmond. A publican named Stammers murdered his wife by hitting her over the head with a bottle of cider.'

'I think I do recall the case. Didn't he then proceed to drink himself silly?'

Cain nodded. 'But not on cider.'

Dr Felling gave a chuckle. 'Let's go into the office and maybe someone will bring us a cup of something.' When they were seated in the small room just inside the entrance to the mortuary, he went on, 'So you've landed this one, have you! It's as strange a tale as I've met for a long time. I imagine you're looking for some sort of a joker. Leaving your victim's body outside a prison shows a perverted sense of humour.'

'You're in no doubt, sir, that it was murder?'

'None at all.'

'So he didn't die as a result of a fall?'

'Not in my opinion. He had a broken neck all right, but he sustained that from a karate chop or something of that nature. Certainly not trom a fall.'

'Can you say how long he'd been dead?'

'That's always a tricky one when some time has elapsed. I made my examination at about four p.m. I gather the body had been found around six a.m. The prison doctor who examined him at the scene reckoned he'd been dead between six and eight hours. I would be prepared to accept that, which means he probably met his death around midnight. Some time between then and six o'clock, his body was dumped outside the prison.'

42

'It's reasonable to assume it was done under cover of darkness,' Cain remarked. 'That would mean in the small hours of the morning.'

'I found nothing in the course of my examination to suggest where he was killed. Forensic may help on that when they take a detailed look at his clothing.'

'I certainly hope they will find something, but . . .' Cain shrugged. 'I shan't be surprised if they don't.'

'Why the pessimism?'

'Because this was obviously a premeditated crime and the murderer will have taken care to cover his tracks.'

'He could still have slipped up somewhere. A lot of murderers do.'

'I know, but I'm not depending on it. Do you happen to know when the coroner is opening his inquest?'

'I gather he'd like to do so as soon as possible and then adjourn until the police have completed their enquiries.'

'I'd better have a word with him,' Cain said. After a pause he went on in a thoughtful voice, 'Would the karate chop that killed Ruding have required expertise?'

'Yes and no. The main requirement is that it should be delivered swiftly and accurately to the front of the neck. It fractures the hyoid bone and causes severe trauma. Vagal inhibition, as in this case, is often the actual cause of death.' He gave Cain a professional look. 'Don't let anyone ever play around with your neck, not even in fun. The vagus nerve can behave unpredictably.'

'I'll remember that,' Cain said with a faint smile.

He would mention it to his wife. She was twenty-two and sixteen years younger than himself and rather given to playful wrestling in the privacy of their home. They had been married just under a year and to date their bliss was still intact. He had had to put up with a good deal of teasing from colleagues when he surrendered his bachelorhood to marry a much younger person. And still more when she became pregnant in the first few months of marriage.

'Well, if that's all, I'll be on my way, Chief Inspector.

I've got another half-dozen post mortems to do before I've earned a gin and tonic. It's been nice running into you again. Let me know if I can help any further.'

As soon as Cain got back to the Yard, he sent for Detective Sergeant Saddler who was to be his sidekick on the enquiry. They had worked as a team before and got on well. Saddler smoked heavily and was overweight, yet remained perversely fit. Perhaps it had something to do with the fact that, like Cain, he never flapped or lost his temper. He felt there were more important things in life than one's job. In his case, playing the saxophone in a group that was never short of bookings in the area where they lived.

'Anything to report, Chris?' Cain asked when his sergeant appeared.

'I've managed to run Mrs Ruding to earth. The dead man's mother, that is. I'm afraid she doesn't like the police. Thinks our only concern is a cover-up. She did let drop that she had been to see Rosa Epton who had been her son's solicitor.'

'Did she say why?'

'She refused to be drawn on that.'

'Maybe I should get in touch with Ms Epton. Have you ever come across her, Chris? She's flint beneath an exterior as sweet as crème caramel. Has a Chinese boyfriend who's also a solicitor.'

'Sounds an exotic dish,' Saddler observed dryly.

'There's a Detective Chief Inspector Cain on the line,' Stephanie said when Rosa answered her telephone the next morning. 'Shall I put him through?'

'Did he say what it was about?' Rosa said as she sought to place the name.

'No. Shall I ask him?'

'Don't bother. I'll find out soon enough.'

'Miss Epton? This is Detective Chief Inspector Cain at Scotland Yard. It's a longish time since we met. I was a detective sergeant and you were the junior partner at Snaith and Epton.'

44

'I still am,' Rosa said, 'so you've obviously done better.'

'I don't think that follows. Anyway, I'm calling you, Miss Epton, because I've been put in charge of enquiries into the death of Edward Ruding.'

'Ah!'

'You represented him at his recent trial, I understand?'

'Yes.'

'So you probably know all about his death.'

'I know what I've read in the papers.'

'I believe Ruding's mother has been to see you.' After a pause in which Rosa said nothing he added, 'I wasn't hiding under your desk, but we've been in touch with her and she told us.' There was a further pause before he went on, 'It seems to me, Miss Epton, that it would be helpful if we met and had a chat.'

'Certainly.'

'As soon as possible. May I come along to your office this afternoon?'

'I'm afraid today is no good.'

'It is rather urgent, Miss Epton. Would you be prepared to see me at your home this evening? Say, around eight thirty?'

'Yes, I'll be there, if it's that urgent. I'll give you my address.'

'I think I already have it. Is it still the flat on Campden Hill?'

'Yes,' Rosa said with a degree of surprise.

As she washed up her supper dishes that evening, she found herself awaiting her visitor with distinct curiosity. She would have liked to have discussed things with either Robin or Peter. But Robin had left the office mid-morning to travel up to Manchester and Peter was on one of his day-trips to the Continent to meet a client who, for financial reasons, couldn't safely set foot in the UK.

It was precisely eight thirty when her doorbell rang and she pressed the button that released the catch on the street door. Her flat was on the third floor and there was no lift.

It was always interesting to see in what condition her visitors arrived. Most needed time to recover their breath and few reached her front door with the spring of a mountain goat.

'Sorry about the stairs,' Rosa said as she opened the door to admit Cain.

'What stairs?' he said with a smile. 'It's good of you to let me disturb your evening and I appreciate it.'

Rosa had recognised him as soon as she opened the door. Moreover, she recalled him as an officer she could trust. That didn't mean you told him everything he would probably like to know. Simply that you didn't have to hide everything and lock up the silver. Whether or not she would have felt flattered by Cain's recent description of her to Sergeant Saddler remained beyond the realm of speculation.

'Would you like a drink?' she said as they went into the living-room.

'I'd love a cup of coffee.'

'I've only got instant.'

'Is there another sort?'

For someone faced with a difficult enquiry, he seemed in an almost carefree mood. Perhaps he knew something that she didn't.

'So what's the urgency?' she said when she returned from the kitchen with two mugs of coffee.

'The urgency is to find a vicious murderer before the trail runs cold.' He pulled a face. 'Except, at the moment, I don't even have a trail to follow. But that's where I'm hoping you can help me.'

'In what way?'

'When you defended Ruding, did he ever give you reason to believe that his life was under threat?'

'I take it you know what his defence was?'

'That he carried out the burglary as an agent of MI5.'

'Yes. But MI5 wouldn't help. Not that that was wholly surprising.'

'But they did help later. They pulled the necessary strings to get him out of prison. I assume you knew that.'

46

'It was what I deduced. I didn't actually know.'

'Didn't he get in touch with you after he was let out?'

'No. At least, not in the way you mean.'

Cain frowned. 'I don't follow.'

'I think he may have been responsible for my being pushed under a tram.'

'A tram?' Cain said in a startled voice. 'Where?'

'In Amsterdam.'

Rosa then went on to relate what had happened on her weekend visit to the city.

'What an extraordinary business. Why should he have wanted to kill you? I simply don't understand.'

'Neither do I. He was obviously determined that I shouldn't come home and start asking questions.'

'And did you start asking questions when you got back?'

'I spoke to Detective Sergeant Crisp, but all he told me was that he'd been instructed to send the papers to the Yard.'

Cain nodded. 'Did you take any other steps?'

'I phoned Colin Kirby, but met with the customary brick-wall response.'

Cain gave a half-smile. 'That figures. MI5 is not very forthcoming in its dealings with outsiders.'

'I wasn't exactly an outsider.'

'From their point of view, you were something worse. You'd been peeping through their keyhole.' After a pause, he went on, 'It's none of my business why Mrs Ruding came to see you, though I confess I find it interesting, but as a result of her visit, do you have any ideas as to who might have killed her son?'

'You have an advocate's art for framing inadmissible questions in an admissible way,' Rosa said with a broad smile.

Cain smiled back. 'Something rubs off when one spends so much time listening in court.'

'But to answer your question,' Rosa went on, 'I gather there's someone called Tam Grigg who mightn't have been sorry to see Eddie Ruding out of the way.'

'Tam Grigg,' Cain said as he made a note of the name.

'I'll see if our computer knows anything about him. Anyone else?'

'No.' She decided not to mention Eddie's brother in Holland. She had referred to the Dutch connection and that would clearly go back to MI5 for their assessment.

She had told Mrs Ruding she would do what she could to find out the truth of her son's death, but saw no reason why the police shouldn't do the donkey work.

Shortly afterwards Cain got up to leave. He thanked her for her time and hospitality and suggested they should keep in touch with each other.

It was about an hour later that her phone rang and she heard Peter's voice on the line.

'I'm still in Brussels,' he said in a resigned voice. 'I thought the meeting would never end. Anyway, every cloud has a silver lining, as every Englishman confidently believes, and I've decided to fly to Amsterdam first thing in the morning and return home from there. I've already searched through the telephone directory and found a V. Ruding who lives in Jutenbergerstraat. I'll try and find out if V stands for Vincent. Keep tomorrow evening free and I'll give you my report. And Rosa?'

'Yes.'

'Don't forget I love you.'

'I'll try and remember,' she said, giving the telephone receiver a happy smile.

Chapter 7

Tam Grigg had always been a keep-fit fanatic and nowadays spent more time than ever in his gymnasium which had all the latest equipment. After a thorough work-out he would dive into the heated swimming pool and do twenty lengths.

These were his extravagances, for unlike most criminals

in his league he didn't squander the fruits of his crimes. He had never lashed out on presents for distant relatives, all of whom had long since given up any hope of a nice new car or a surprise holiday in the Canaries. Even his wife, from whom he was now separated, seldom received more than a hideous piece of costume jewellery after one of his hauls. For him, money was for investing in property; in bricks and mortar.

He had a large house in the Surrey stockbroker belt which was comfortably furnished, though in eccentric taste. The gymnasium, swimming pool and Jacuzzi, which he had added, had cost him a few thousand pounds (near enough a hundred thousand to be exact), but he regarded that as money well spent. He didn't mix with his neighbours, who wrote him off as a vulgar *nouveau riche* – not that he was bothered by that as long as they kept their distance.

As a child, he had often been asked what Tam was short for.

'It's not short for nothing,' he would reply in a pugnacious tone which deterred further questions. 'It's as good a name as yours.'

On the afternoon following DCI Cain's visit to Rosa, he was waiting to be picked up by his cousin, Alex Cartwright, who was his closest associate. His own car was in the garage for a service. It was a fairly new Jaguar and, in his view, shouldn't have needed a service. The fact that the garage had arranged to fetch it and likewise return it at the end of the day did nothing to ease his sense of frustration. He didn't want some sharp-eyed mechanic giving his property the once-over when he brought it back.

'Leave it in the drive,' he had said tersely. Beneath his breath he had added, 'And piss off.'

As he waited for Alex to arrive he found himself thinking back to his childhood days in South London and to the Ruding family who lived next door. Mrs Ruding had been a real pain in the arse. No wonder her husband, the Flying Dutchman, had flown. But he had got on all right with Eddie, largely because Eddie always did what he told him. Then when Eddie grew up to be an accomplished cat burglar, Tam had renewed contact with him. In fact their paths had crossed again in prison and Tam had given him a helping hand when he came out. Eddie had skills that Tam could use. It was a pity they'd no longer be available.

Tam had read most of the newspaper accounts of Eddie's demise. It was an event on which he felt he should be fully briefed. So far there had been nothing in any of them to cause him any concern.

He saw Alex's car turn into the drive and was waiting outside by the time it pulled up at the front door.

'You don't want to come in, do you?' he said to his cousin and got into the car without waiting for a reply.

'It'd be a gesture to attend Eddie's funeral,' Alex said after they had driven some way in silence.

'It'd be a bloody silly one.'

'Well, at least we can send some flowers.'

'That'd be almost as stupid. The police'll not only be checking the mourners, but the names of those who sent wreaths.'

'Do you think so?'

'I'm darned sure of it. And the last thing I want is to be connected with Eddie's death.'

'There's no reason why you should be, Tam.'

'I hope that's right, but Eddie's mother's the sort of spiteful old bat to make a bit of mischief.'

'What'll you tell the police if they come asking questions?'

Tam gave his cousin a surprised look. 'Depends on the questions. You know my motto, never give them aggro if you can avoid it, because two can play at that.' He paused before adding, 'But that don't mean you help the bastards unless it helps you too.'

Peter caught an early flight from Brussels to Amsterdam and was in the city by eight thirty. He took a taxi from the airport to Jutenbergerstraat and paid it off outside the address he had found for V. Ruding in the telephone directory. There appeared to be four floors of flats, each with its own bell push and beside it the occupant's name. But no V. Ruding. Then he noticed a name card beneath all the others on which was printed the word *concierge* in faded letters. He pressed the bell and waited for the intercom to crackle into life.

It did so almost immediately and an echoing male voice said something in Dutch.

'I wish to talk to Mr Vincent Ruding,' Peter said. 'Can you help me please?'

'Who is it?' the voice asked in English.

'My name's Chen.'

There was a pause before the door buzzed open.

'Down here,' a voice called out as Peter closed the door behind him.

A flight of stone stairs led to the basement and he descended. A man was standing at an open door at the bottom, observing him. He was sturdily built with a bullet-shaped head, bald on top and with a surround of reddish bristles. He hadn't shaved recently and was dressed in a pair of dirty jeans and a white vest several sizes too small.

'Are you Vincent Ruding?' Peter asked.

'Who are you?' the man replied suspiciously.

'My name's Peter Chen.'

'That doesn't tell me anything. What do you want?'

'I want to talk to Vincent Ruding.'

'What about?'

'His brother's death.'

It seemed to Peter that every bristle on the man's head and face stiffened with further suspicion.

'You'd better come in,' he said at length. 'My wife's gone to the market.'

He led the way into a room where a parrot in a cage screeched a welcome. Or it could have been a curse. The man addressed it in Dutch and it turned its back on them and picked up a nut.

'I take it you are Vincent Ruding?' Peter said when they were both seated.

51

'What if I am?'

'You know about your brother's death?'

'Look, Mr Chen, we'll get on faster if you tell me your business. What do *you* know about my brother's death and how did you find me?'

Peter was sure that the man sitting opposite him had not been one of those with Eddie at the café in Leidseplein. That didn't, of course, mean he was ignorant of his brother's visit to Amsterdam.

'Does the name Rosa Epton mean anything to you?' Peter said. Ruding shook his head and Peter went on, 'She's a London solicitor and she's represented your brother a couple of times, including at his last court appearance. She also happens to be my girlfriend.'

'My wife's Javanese,' Ruding said with a grin. 'Holland is full of orientals from the old Dutch East Indies. Where are you from?'

'Hong Kong.'

'Anyway, you've still not said why you're here.'

'My girlfriend wants to find out the truth behind your brother's death. Did you know he'd been released from prison soon after his conviction?'

'That was legit. They had to let him out. One favour deserved another.'

'Is that what Eddie told you?'

'Yes.'

'Did you see him not long before his death?'

Ruding picked at his teeth with a matchstick, watched by Peter and the parrot.

'He was over in Amsterdam last month. He got in touch and we met.'

'Did he say what brought him here?'

'It was some people he was mixed up with. I can't tell you more than that.' Peter was wondering if he meant 'can't' or 'won't', when Ruding went on, 'They weren't anything to do with me. I didn't meet them.'

'Did Eddie tell you who they were?'

'No.'

'You must have got some clue?'

'All I know is that they weren't either Dutch or English. They could have been German.'

'What makes you say that?'

'Eddie mentioned someone called Reiner.'

'Might Reiner have been an East German?' Peter asked as he plucked his lower lip with a thoughtful expression.

'East or West, take your pick,' Ruding remarked with a shrug.

'How many times did you see him when he was here?'

'Only once. And we spoke on the phone once.'

'Were you surprised when he got in touch with you?'

'Why should I have been surprised?'

'Didn't you think he'd just been sent to prison for five years?'

'Oh, I see what you mean. Yes, I suppose I was a bit surprised.'

'Was Eddie ever mixed up in the spying business?'

'Eddie, a spy? He was mixed up in so many things from time to time, I suppose he could have been, but if he was, he never told me. But then he wouldn't have, would he?'

'Did he say anything about his trial when he was here?'

'He said your girlfriend had done her best for him, but the judge was a real bastard and had been out to get him from the start. He was pretty sore about it as he felt he'd been sold down the river. But everything turned out all right in the end. Well . . . all right as far as his not being kept in prison was concerned.'

'Have you any idea who might have killed him?'

'None. You won't find an answer to that question this side of the North Sea.'

'Why are you so certain of that?'

For the first time Vincent Ruding looked put out. 'It stands to reason, doesn't it? He met his death in England and it's in England you have to look for his killer.'

It had become apparent to Peter that Ruding was well

briefed on his brother's death. He had either read all the English newspaper accounts or he was in touch with someone on the spot. Peter was inclined to think that the second was more likely.

'I understand Eddie lived with his mother?'

'That's right.'

'Your mother, in fact.'

'I'm not in touch with her. Haven't been for years. I don't even think of her as my mother any more.' He got up and stretched. 'I reckon I've answered enough questions for one day. Anyway, I've got work to do.'

'It's good of you to have given me so much of your time,' Peter said as he walked toward the door which Ruding was holding open.

After Peter had departed, Ruding stood for a while deep in thought. Then, returning to the room in which they had talked, he exchanged knowing winks with the parrot.

Colin Kirby's career had been under a shadow ever since the Bilak fiasco, for not only had he disregarded a number of instructions about the use of outsiders, but the whole exercise had been a disastrous and embarrassing failure. Its main purpose had been thwarted and Ruding had been caught red-handed. Worse still, he had called on the Security Service to come to his rescue and testify at his trial. That, of course, had been out of the question.

As a result of all this, Kirby's superiors had made known their displeasure and his future had been put under review. The fact remained, however, that he was an effective operational officer, provided his natural inclination to act as a loner could be curbed.

He was now in his mid-forties and had come to the UK with the highest credentials from the Rhodesian police force soon after the country had become Zimbabwe. For a while he had worked for a private security company, but had then been recruited by MI5. His boss in the Rhodesian Police had links with the Service and had warmly recommended him.

54

He was unmarried and lived in the basement flat of a house in Pimlico, which had the advantage of affording greater privacy than the other flats in the building which were served by the main street door and a common staircase. He had his own front door which was reached by a short flight of steps leading down from the pavement above. This was especially important as it meant his visitors could come and go without being seen by the other occupants of the house. He could hold briefing sessions with the likes of Eddie Ruding which wouldn't have been practicable in the office.

He was on nodding terms with those who lived in the flats above his and had made it his business to find out more about them than they would have appreciated. For their part, they knew him as a middle-grade civil servant, which, in a sense, he was. He went off to work every morning and returned around seven o'clock most evenings. They knew nothing of the visitors who flitted up and down the basement steps. And if they did happen to encounter someone arriving or departing, they thought nothing of it. He was entitled to entertain friends as much as they were. And very much in his favour, he didn't make any noise.

On the evening of the day that Peter spent in Amsterdam, Kirby arrived home at around seven thirty. He had had special locks fitted to the front door and windows. A basement flat was inevitably more vulnerable than those on the upper floors, though, to Colin Kirby, the advantages overcame the disadvantages.

Once inside he double-locked the door behind him and went straight to the drinks cupboard. After a large Scotch, followed by another, he felt better. Life hadn't been much fun of late and he hated being under a cloud. He took pride in his work and found the cloak-and-dagger element stimulating.

He still considered Eddie Ruding had been the right man for the Bilak job, which should have gone off without a hitch. Nobody could blame him for dropping into the arms of a waiting policeman: that was sheer bad luck. What was inexcusable was his theft of £6000. That was greedy opportunism. Then, on top of that, to try and involve the service added insult to injury. In the circumstances, he was lucky not to have been left to rot in prison. Except that he was likely to have made more trouble inside than out, though nobody knew at that stage he was going to end up dead within a few weeks.

As he helped himself to a third Scotch, he wondered what he could do to restore his position. He hoped he was too valuable to be put out to grass – or its equivalent, a transfer to a backwater desk job. The fact that nothing had happened as yet was in itself hopeful, but not conclusive. Presumably the powers-that-be were waiting to see the outcome of the enquiry into Ruding's death. For the time being the whole matter was what the lawyers called *sub judice*.

He walked into the kitchen and poured away the remainder of his drink. He always knew when he had had enough, not that he ever got drunk.

He went into the bedroom and changed into a track suit, after which he washed his face and cleaned his teeth. He had just finished when the front doorbell rang. He peered through the peephole to make sure it was the person he was expecting.

'Hi,' he said, opening the door to admit his visitor and closing it again quickly. 'Come on in.'

Chapter 8

Detective Chief Inspector Cain let out a sigh as he gazed at his file on the Ruding enquiry. Its growth in no way reflected the progress of the investigation.

He had personally interviewed Rosa Epton, Colin Kirby, Detective Sergeant Crisp and Tam Grigg, but had so far failed to find any fruitful lead. He had also had Clive Fox phoning him at all hours.

Grigg remained a suspect, but he wasn't the sort of man to break down and confess, and without a confession Cain didn't think he was going to get very far. A motive for the killing was what he needed more than anything. Why had somebody murdered Ruding and deposited his body outside the prison in which he had recently spent a short time? Cain reasoned that the need to kill Ruding had arisen after his release. What he had to find out was what Eddie had been up to between his release and his death – a matter of four weeks. He had been to Amsterdam and had apparently been associated with an attempt on Rosa Epton's life. Pushing somebody under a tram seemed a bizarre way of killing them – and yet murders that looked like accidents were often the most successful.

He drew the file toward him and opened it at Colin Kirby's statement. Kirby could be said to have had some sort of motive for murder, but would he have been likely to have gone to such trouble to engineer Ruding's release from prison simply to kill him? The answer had to be no.

It was at this point that his phone rang.

'Is that Chief Inspector Cain?' a voice asked nervously.

'Cain speaking.'

'I can help you,' the voice went on in a breathless rush. 'I think I know who killed Eddie Ruding.'

'Who is speaking?' Cain asked, reaching for his pen and a piece of paper.

'Let's just say I was a friend of Eddie's.'

'Where can we meet and have a talk?'

'Not at your place. I'm not coming there.'

'You suggest somewhere.'

'Know that bombed-out church in Soho?'

'St Anne's, do you mean?'

'That's the one. It has seats in the old churchyard. I'll be waiting there in one hour's time.'

Before Cain could say anything further, his caller had

57

disconnected. He glanced at his watch. It was just after four o'clock. He had ample time to get to the rendezvous. He knew the area well, having been stationed at West End Central as a detective constable.

He arrived in the churchyard a few minutes before five and sat down on the only seat that wasn't occupied. He had hardly done so when an old woman festooned with plastic bags joined him and produced a bottle from one of them. She had a good, long drink and offered it to him. He thanked her but declined, whereupon she began to abuse him as though he were responsible for the misfortunes of all the vagrants in the area.

He got up and walked toward the tower which was all that was left of the church. There was nobody around who looked as if he was waiting for someone. Indeed, nobody so much as gave him a glance. As for the bag lady, she had sunk into a state of drowsy, if still bellicose, muttering.

By five thirty, Cain had decided that his telephone caller was not going to show up. The whole thing could have been a hoax and yet somehow he didn't believe that it was. In any event there was nothing he could do about it. Maybe the caller would get in touch again. He hoped so, for he was ready to follow any lead he was offered.

He went into a callbox and phoned his wife to cheer himself up.

Snaith and Epton's offices were one floor up from ground level, their main entrance opening on to a small, dingy landing with a flight of stairs leading down to the street door of the building.

On that particular afternoon, Rosa was the last to leave and had the responsibility of locking up. It was about six fifteen and the office closed officially at five thirty.

As she reached the pavement, she was aware of a man moving out of the shadow of a doorway on the opposite side of the street. He came hurrying over to her.

'Miss Epton? You are Miss Epton, aren't you?' he said

in an ingratiating tone. 'I know you, but you don't know me.'

Rosa eyed him without enthusiasm. He didn't look like a mugger, or to be more precise he didn't look as if he was about to mug her, which was different. He was short with sharp, foxy features. Rosa maintained her guard which involved changing her grip on her briefcase so that she could use it to clout him if he made an aggressive movement.

'I saw you at the Old Bailey at Eddie Ruding's trial,' he went on with what was intended to be a reassuring smile. 'I was in the public gallery. I attended as a friend of Eddie's. I can probably help you find his murderer.'

'What's your name?' Rosa asked after a pause.

'Call me Joe.'

'Joe what?'

'Just Joe.'

'There's a café round the corner,' Rosa said. 'Let's go there.'

'Excellent idea,' he said keenly. 'I could do with a cup of tea.'

When they were seated with tea in front of them, Rosa went on, 'By rights you should take your information to the police. They're investigating Eddie Ruding's death.'

'Yes, Detective Chief Inspector Cain, isn't it? As a matter of fact I did call him this afternoon and we fixed a rendezvous, but then I chickened out.' Despite his shabby appearance, he was articulate and well spoken. 'You don't mind if I smoke, do you?' he enquired as he produced a tin of tobacco and a packet of cigarette papers from his pocket. Rosa watched him roll one and light it. 'Yes, I'm afraid I let the Chief Inspector down. I hope he's not still hanging around waiting for me. The fact is that after I'd called him, I realised I'd been a bit hasty. On the whole the police are not my best friends and though Chief Inspector Cain may be a nice enough man, he's still a policeman. So I decided to skip our meeting and come and see you instead. If you feel you should pass on what I tell you to the police, that's something we can discuss later.'

'You say you were a friend of Eddie's . . .'

'Perhaps associate would describe our relationship better. By which I mean, we weren't social friends.'

Presumably that's a prim way of saying they were partners in crime on occasions, Rosa reflected as she waited for him to go on.

'I wonder if I might have another cup of tea?' he said. 'It's so rare these days to get a decent cup and this is delicious. It has a proper flavour.'

'You were saying,' Rosa prompted him when the second cup arrived.

'I saw Eddie the week after he came out of prison. I could scarcely believe my eyes as I hadn't expected to see him again for several years. He said they'd had to let him out, otherwise he could have raised hell. Mind you, I took that with a pinch of salt; Eddie was always prone to touches of self-importance. But there he was as large as life and as free as a bird. I asked him what he had lined up for the future and he said he had a number of irons in the fire and that one in particular appealed to him. "I think I've got a nice little meal ticket, Joe," was what he said. "One that should keep me comfy for quite a while, if I play my cards right." "Tell me about it, Eddie," I said. "And have you mess up my scam, Joe? Not likely." He added that he also had other business to attend to and that he'd probably be going abroad. Eddie loved talking big,' Joe added with a reminiscent smile. 'I expect you found that out, too.'

'Is this what you were going to tell Chief Inspector Cain?'

'Near enough,' he said with one of his small, wary smiles.

'And you believe it helps identify Eddie's murderer?'

'It's an important part of the jigsaw,' he said in a slightly huffed tone. 'Obviously the police should be trying to reconstruct the time between his release from prison and his being found at the foot of the prison wall with a broken neck.'

'I'm sure that's what Chief Inspector Cain is seeking to do.' She looked at her watch. 'Well, if that's all, Joe . . .'

'I could do with another cup of tea,' he said hopefully.

'All right, but I hope you won't mind if I leave you to drink it on your own.'

He sighed. 'There is something else I can tell you,' he said in a confidential whisper when his third cup of tea had arrived. 'You're not in a great hurry, are you?'

It was Rosa's turn to sigh. It was clear that Joe was intent on spinning things out for as long as possible. Certainly as long as the tea lasted. She felt that what he had told her so far hardly merited the cost of three cups of tea.

'OK, tell me. What else?'

He leaned across the table as if to add weight to his words.

'I don't suppose the name Grigg means anything to you?'

'Tam Grigg, do you mean?'

'Oh, you have heard of him. He and Eddie grew up in the same street.'

'I know.'

'Grigg is thoroughly bad news, Miss Epton. He's utterly ruthless.'

'So?'

'When Eddie told me he had a nice little meal ticket lined up, I reckoned he meant he'd got something on someone.' He shot her a sly glance. 'Follow me?'

'Blackmail, you mean?'

'Exactly. Moreover, I reckon it was Grigg at the receiving end.'

Rosa looked sceptical. 'In the first place, what would have been the nature of the blackmail? And in the second, would Eddie have dared?'

'Good questions, good questions. Grigg's masterminded a number of robberies in recent years. Supposing Eddie was in possession of evidence that could nail him, the police would be so pleased they'd recommend him for the OBE.'

'Surely, he'd be asking for the chop if he grassed on Tam Grigg?' Rosa said.

'Which he got,' Joe replied with a note of triumph. 'Eddie's release from prison was his undoing, if you follow

61

me.' Rosa didn't, as her expression showed, and Joe continued, 'It went to his head. Made him over-confident. He believed he could handle any situation, even blackmailing Grigg.'

Rosa's expression remained dubious. It was true that in her dealings with him, he had never seemed to lack self-confidence. Perhaps his release from jail *had* given him inflated ideas about what he could achieve.

'I can see you're with me,' Joe said keenly, so that, for a moment, she thought he was going to ask for another cup of tea. Instead, he jumped up and said in a tone that implied she had been keeping him, 'Well, I have to be going. I think we ought to keep in touch with each other. I'll call you again in a day or so.' Leaving Rosa to pay for all the cups of tea, he moved toward the door. A thought apparently struck him, for he suddenly came back. 'There's certain to be a reward, isn't there?'

He didn't wait for an answer, but turned on his heel and left the café.

In the event he resurfaced in Rosa's life sooner than she expected or wanted, and in a manner quite unforeseen.

Chapter 9

Rosa was always alerted when she arrived in the office to be greeted by one of Stephanie's and-now-what-have-you-been-up-to looks. This is what happened the next morning.

'You're needed at Bayswater Magistrates' Court,' she said as Rosa came through the door. 'As soon as possible,' she added. 'The phone began ringing immediately I plugged in this morning.'

'I don't have any cases at Bayswater,' Rosa said with a frown.

'You have now, if I got the message right. There's a

Joseph Gillfroy up on a loitering with intent charge. He'd like you there to defend him.'

'I've never heard of Joseph Gillfroy . . . unless . . . unless it's Joe who waylaid me outside the office yesterday evening. Can you get me the court, Steph?'

It didn't take long to confirm that Joseph Gillfroy was indeed Joe and was asking urgently for her attendance.

'OK, tell him I'll come along,' she said to the official to whom she was speaking. 'Sorry if I sounded a bit dumb, but I didn't know his name was Gillfroy. As far as I'm concerned he's plain Joe.'

'I wish I didn't know him at all. If he's told me once, he's told me a dozen times that it's Gillfroy with two Ls. Anyway, he'll be happy to know you're on your way, Miss Epton. The sooner we can get shot of him, the better for my blood pressure.'

Before Rosa could ask what exactly Joe had been up to, the receiver at the other end had been replaced.

It was with more curiosity than relish that she set out. It was lucky for Joe that she wasn't due in court elsewhere that morning.

She had spent the previous evening with Peter when he had given her an account of his visit to Vincent Ruding and she had told him of Joe's sudden appearance in the story.

'I should think you can write him off as a not very reliable informant,' Peter had observed. 'He's obviously after a reward and you'll probably find that everything he told you is either thirdhand or pure invention. If you encourage him, I can envisage his becoming a thorough nuisance.'

After they had had dinner, Peter had accompanied her home and they had made love. By midnight he had departed and she was in bed and asleep.

Rosa had often likened London's magistrates' courts to busy stores on a sales day. People milled about, some looking lost and bemused, others anxious and others again purposeful and determined. It's rare, however, to see anyone looking relaxed.

'Ah, Miss Epton,' Joe said, jumping up from a bench in the corner of the jailer's office. 'I confess that I never anticipated that we'd meet again so soon. This is all most unfortunate.'

He was unshaven and looked foxier than he had the previous day.

'You'd better tell me what's happened,' Rosa said, sitting down beside him. 'Incidentally, I gather your name is Gillfroy.'

'Yes, with two Ls. I'm very particular about the spelling.' He gazed about him with an air of distaste as if he found the whole scene totally alien.

'Forget the spelling,' Rosa said briskly, 'and tell me what you've done.'

'I went down an alleyway and was standing there when a policeman came up.'

'What were you doing in the alleyway? And don't tell me it was to answer a call of nature!'

Joe gave her a hurt look. 'I just wanted to have a bit of a reconnoitre.'

'What of?'

'The back of a shop.'

'What sort of shop?'

'A jeweller's.'

Rosa sighed. Why couldn't it have been a baker's or a launderette? Loitering in the vicinity of a jeweller's shop was like lighting a match to examine a keg of dynamite.

'What time was this?'

'About two o'clock this morning.'

'And why did you want to reconnoitre there?'

He looked away and said sulkily, 'I just did. I had an idea it could be helpful.'

'With a view to breaking in at a later date?'

'I'm not a common burglar,' he said stiffly.

Rosa felt her patience was being stretched. 'I think the best course will be to ask for a remand. Until I know all the facts, I can't possibly defend you, though I'm bound to

64

say that it sounds very much as if you'll eventually have to plead guilty.' She gave him a stern look. 'Do you have any previous convictions?'

'Just a few,' he muttered. 'Nothing serious, mind you. Nothing for violence.'

Just then a young man in a sports jacket and brown corduroy trousers approached the bench where they were sitting.

'I'm DC Hornby,' he said. 'Are you defending Gillfroy?'

'Yes. My name's Rosa Epton.'

'The prosecution will be asking for a remand,' he went on. 'I'd been hoping we could have the case disposed of today, but it seems further enquiries have to be made.'

'May I ask what further enquiries?'

'You may ask, but I'm not at liberty to disclose their nature,' he replied.

Rosa had never taken to overbearing police officers, particularly when they were still wet behind the ears.

'I shall be applying for bail and for the earliest possible disposal of the case,' she said.

'Is it likely to be a plea of guilty?'

'Wait and see.'

DC Hornby gave her a sour look and turned away. Shortly afterwards Rosa took her seat in court.

Neither of the two regular stipendiary magistrates was on duty that day; instead, an acting magistrate was presiding. This meant, in practice, a barrister who aspired to be appointed to a permanent post and who was being tried out for suitability. In Rosa's experience acting magistrates came in two sizes. There were those who were aggressively determined to show they were in complete control and didn't need advice or guidance from anyone, and those who hid their nervousness behind a façade of almost fawning politeness to everyone in court and who consulted the clerk on every occasion.

Mr Henshaw, who was presiding that day, belonged to the second school. Rosa had barely got into court before

65

he broke off what he was doing and gave her a courtly bow which she returned while on the move to her seat. They knew each other slightly and Rosa regarded him as an amiable ditherer. She was surprised to find him sitting as a magistrate and couldn't feel that he would make the grade. She noticed that the clerk already wore a fraught expression and the jailer, who marshalled defendants in and out of court, had the martyred air of a Saint Sebastian facing more than his usual quota of arrows.

There was only one other person in the lawyers' row and that was a preoccupied young man with a mountain of files in front of him which he appeared to be trying to put in some order. Rosa decided that he had to be from the Crown Prosecution Service.

'What case are you in?' he hissed as Rosa sat down.

'Gillfroy. I gather you're asking for a remand.'

'Are we? Oh, good! Gillfroy, did you say?'

'With two Ls.'

'Yes, I have the file here,' he said with a note of triumph.

'I see you're in the case of Gillfroy, Miss Epton,' the magistrate said, examining the slip of paper conveying the information which the usher had just handed him. 'I'm sure you'd like to get away as soon as possible. If it suits everyone, we can take your case now.' He glanced from clerk to jailer to the public at large as if for their approval.

'That would be most helpful, sir,' Rosa said. 'I understand the prosecution is seeking a remand. I have no objection to that, though I wish to apply for bail on behalf of my client.'

'No reason why Mr Gillfroy shouldn't have bail, is there, Mr Todmarsh?' the magistrate said, turning to the young man from the CPS.

The jailer, meanwhile, was making semaphore signals to the clerk, who suddenly realised that Joe was still somewhere outside.

'Bring in Gillfroy,' the clerk said.

'Indeed, yes,' the magistrate said anxiously.

Joe entered the dock and sat down.

66

'Stand up,' hissed the jailer.

'Please be seated, Mr Gillfroy,' said the magistrate.

'I think he should stand while I put the charge to him,' the clerk said firmly.

Mr Henshaw nodded. 'Yes, of course.'

Five minutes later Joe had been remanded on bail for three weeks. Rosa reckoned that in his efforts to please everyone, the magistrate had managed to make the hearing last twice as long as it need have done.

After a final exchange of bows and being effusively thanked for her help to the court, Rosa slipped gratefully away, her sympathies with those who had to bear with Mr Henshaw for the rest of the day. Once the bail formalities were completed, she and Joe left the building.

'What about a cup of tea?' Joe said, when they were outside.

'I must get back to my office,' Rosa replied firmly. 'But phone and make an appointment to come and see me. And don't leave it to the last moment.' She was thoughtful for a time. 'What exactly were you doing at the jeweller's shop, if it wasn't an act preparatory to breaking in?'

'I wanted to see how well protected it was.'

'I dare say, but why?'

'Because it's owned by Tam Grigg, that's why. The jewellery business is just a front. You could say it's a front for a laundry. A place to launder money.' He gave Rosa a sly grin.

It occurred to her as she drove back to the office that Joe Gillfroy, with his two Ls, knew a good deal about Tam Grigg. About Eddie Ruding, too. In each case more than she knew about him.

She wondered if she was being used, but if so, by whom and to what purpose? She arrived back at her office without having found any satisfactory answers. Instinct told her, however, that Joe Gillfroy, of whom she had never heard twenty-four hours before, was set to become a permanent irritant in her life.

Chapter 10

It was toward the end of the afternoon when Stephanie informed Rosa that Mrs Ruding wished to speak to her on the phone.

'It's Mrs Charlotte Ruding,' the familiar voice announced when the connection was made. Her prim telephone manner bore small relation to the red-haired cockney matriarch who had sat in Rosa's office a few days earlier.

'Good afternoon, Mrs Ruding,' Rosa said in a guarded tone. 'I'm afraid I don't yet have any information to give you.'

'It's me what's called to give you some,' came the reply. 'I've 'eard from a good source that my Eddie met Grigg the evening before 'e was killed.'

'Where did you hear that?'

'From a good source, like I say. Somebody who knows them both, but doesn't want to get embroiled.'

'Where did they meet?'

'In a pub in the Walworth Road. Early evening, sevenish. What's more they left together. It's proof that Grigg murdered my Eddie.'

Rosa forebore to point out that it was no such thing, though it could turn out to be a piece of useful evidence.

'Is your source able to say what they were talking about in the pub?'

'No, except they seemed kinda thick.'

'Thick?'

'Like a couple of peas out of the same pod,' Mrs Ruding said with a touch of impatience.

'Doesn't sound as if Grigg had murder in mind,' Rosa observed.

'You don't know 'im. 'E's crafty. 'E'd kill 'is own mother if it suited 'im. And if she was still alive. I've told you 'ow my Eddie fell under 'is influence. 'E was too easily led astray. That was 'is downfall. I used to tell 'im so, but 'e only laughed. 'E reckoned 'e could look after 'isself and look where it landed 'im.'

'I'm sure the police would be interested in your information, Mrs Ruding.'

'You can tell 'em, if you want.'

'They'd want to know your source.'

''E won't be embroiled with the police. I've told you that.'

'Is it somebody you know personally?'

'I know 'e's reliable.'

'But do you know him? Is he a friend? Or was he a friend of Eddie's?'

''E was more like an acquaintance of Eddie's.'

'Did he speak to Eddie in the pub?'

'Eddie didn't see 'im. 'E was too busy talking to that Grigg.'

Rosa knew that if she passed the information on to Cain as it stood, his immediate reaction would be to visit Mrs Ruding and put pressure on her to reveal the name of her source. It would serve the red-haired old bat right, though Rosa doubted whether the whole of Scotland Yard could get her to talk if she didn't wish to. A sudden thought crossed her mind.

'Do you know Joe Gillfroy?' she asked.

There was a pause before Mrs Ruding replied.

'I think I 'ave 'eard the name.'

'Is he the source of your information?'

'I'm not saying anything. 'Ear this, Miss Epton. If the Lord 'isself came down from 'eaven and told me Grigg didn't kill my Eddie, I'd 'ave to say, "Sorry, Lord, but I don't believe you." ' She paused and went on, 'Grigg did it and I want to see 'im put away for life. The pity is they can't 'ang 'im.'

DCI Cain went to MI5 headquarters at six o'clock that evening to keep an appointment with a man named John Decker who was Colin Kirby's superior officer.

Apart from the various security checks before being

69

admitted, Cain always found the building itself oppressive. It was as if its vast store of secret information inhibited everyone who worked there. Doors looked more forbiddingly closed than they did in other buildings and staff hurried along corridors as if not wishing to be caught in the open. Visitors were viewed with wariness as if no number of checks would make them welcome. At least this was always Cain's impression on the few occasions he had called there.

Not that there was anything unfriendly about John Decker when he reached his office.

'Let me offer you a drink, Chief Inspector,' he said affably. Walking over to a corner cupboard, he went on, 'The choice is somewhat limited, I'm afraid. Cyprus sherry or Australian white wine. You can tell we're patriotically pro-Commonwealth.'

'Wine, please,' Cain said.

Pouring out two glasses, Decker returned to his desk.

'So what's it about this time?' he asked, as he sat down.

'Colin Kirby.'

'That much I could have guessed. Cheers,' he said, lifting his glass. 'May all your investigations reach successful conclusions.'

'I'll be content if the current one does,' Cain remarked with a sigh.

'What is it about Kirby that's worrying you?'

'I find him something of an enigma.'

'In what way?'

'On the two occasions I've interviewed him, I've had the feeling he's not being open and frank. It's as if he looks at every aspect of each question I put to him before deciding how to answer.'

'That could be his training. We're taught to guard our tongues in this business and not make glib replies. And certainly not to accept them when they're given to us.' Decker took a sip of wine and put his glass down in a thoughtful manner. 'One should also remember that Kirby

70

grew up under different culture, namely in Rhodesia that was, when the white man had things pretty much his own way. He wasn't bothered by all the bureaucratic constraints we suffer from in this country. My own impression is that he has never really adapted to life in the UK. He's remained a bit of a loner. But there've never been any grumbles about his work until the Ruding affair. He knows he overstepped the mark and I believe he feels suitably chastened by what's followed. I'm reasonably confident he won't step out of line again. If I wasn't, he wouldn't still be here.' He gave Cain a quizzical look. 'You don't regard him as a serious suspect in your enquiry, do you?'

Cain didn't immediately reply. Then he said, 'Let's say I have no evidence against him, but instinct tells me that Ruding would have been in touch with him after his release from prison.'

'Have you asked Kirby about that?'

'Yes, and he denies it.'

'But you don't believe him?'

'I have reservations.'

'I can see that Ruding might have tried to get in touch with Kirby, but not the other way about. It was all over as far as Colin was concerned. The operation had become fouled up, which wasn't his fault, and we had subsequently done the fair thing by Ruding. And I don't mind telling you, it took some fixing. The Home Office has never been the most flexible of government departments and they weren't a bit happy over what had happened.'

'When did you first hear about the burglary at Bilak's flat?'

'Not until Ruding was coming up for trial and his solicitor wanted Kirby to give evidence. That, of course, was out of the question.'

'And it was at that point Kirby came to you?'

'Yes. I suppose he suddenly realised he was getting out of his depth and it was time to enlist help before the water rose any higher.' Decker grimaced. 'Our first hope was that

Ruding might be acquitted on some technicality or another, even if his arrest did seem like a classic fair cop. If he'd not taken the money, he might still have talked his way out of it, but that sank all his chances.'

'Why didn't Kirby come to you sooner?'

'That's being wise after the event. He knew he'd exceeded his authority in mounting the operation the way he did, so it was natural he should keep his own counsel for as long as he could, hoping all the while it would come right in the end without his having to involve others. That's understandable, surely?'

'Perhaps,' Cain said doubtfully.

He hadn't come expecting to be handed a bagful of clues, but hoping rather that Decker would say something which opened up a fresh avenue of enquiry. Instead of which, the MI5 man had used the interview to defend his colleague with considerable subtlety.

'I can't see what motive Kirby could have had to murder Ruding,' Decker now went on. 'Nobody in their right mind would suggest it was because Ruding had made a cock-up of the burglary, though Kirby had every reason to feel angry about that. But it doesn't make sense to suggest it provided Kirby with a motive to murder him.'

'What about the code book that Ruding was supposed to steal?'

'What about it?'

'Did you subsequently get hold of it?'

Cain thought at first that Decker wasn't going to reply, but then he shrugged and said, 'For what it's worth, the answer's no. As you're aware, Bilak fled immediately afterwards and not surprisingly took any incriminating papers with him. We weren't off the mark quick enough.'

'Whose fault was that?'

Decker frowned. 'What do you mean?'

'It was Kirby's fault,' Cain went on. 'He didn't come to you with the truth until it was too late. Bilak had decamped, leaving his flat as bare as Mother Hubbard's cupboard. Bare, that is, of anything that might have interested you.' He paused. 'The question is whether Kirby is a knave or a fool.'

He left Decker looking particularly thoughtful. He would have liked to examine Kirby's personal file, but knew it was pointless to ask if he might scrutinise it. He might eventually get to see it after a bureaucratic wrestling match. He didn't even know if it contained any material that might assist him. Nevertheless he would like to browse through it.

For all that Decker had said, Cain remained sceptical of Kirby's role. Poor old MI5 had taken a bashing in recent times with various allegations against its members, including the suggestion that its one-time Director-General had been a Russian spy. It seemed possible that Kirby was a double agent and that Ruding had somehow discovered this.

Cain wondered if he was being fanciful. Mixing with spooks could have this effect if one was not careful.

Chapter 11

Three days later Eddie Ruding's funeral took place.

The coroner had opened his inquest and adjourned it after hearing formal evidence of identification and cause of death, to enable police enquiries to take their course. He didn't immediately release the body for burial, but did so eventually after pressure from Eddie's mother in the form of two indignant letters. By then he was satisfied that Dr Felling's post mortem findings couldn't be seriously disputed and that Eddie couldn't have died as a result of falling from the prison wall. Moreover, what could be more conclusive than the word of the prison governor, who said that Eddie wasn't an inmate of the prison at the time of his death?

Mrs Ruding phoned Rosa to give her details of the funeral. She didn't ask whether she proposed to attend, but implied that she was expecting a good turn-out.

Rosa discussed the matter with Peter who suggested they should both attend. When she mentioned it to Robin, however, he made it clear that he didn't approve.

'In what capacity would you be going?' he asked in a tone that warned Rosa to watch her step.

'Well, he was my client . . .'

'*Was*,' Robin observed. 'If we attended the funerals of all our ex-clients, it would be a full-time occupation—'

'And there was the incident in Amsterdam.'

'What else?'

'Mrs Ruding is now a client.'

'I've yet to understand what professional service we are able to offer her.'

It wasn't often that Robin was able to discomfit her – or even tried to do so. But the fact she respected him as her senior partner and was fond of him as a person wasn't making their exchange any easier.

'So you don't think I ought to go?' she said.

'I can't see any point in your going, but, if you can spare the time, it's up to you. I don't feel partners should dictate to one another. Even a senior to a junior.' The remark was accompanied by a faint smile.

'I do so see your point of view,' Rosa said, 'but I'd like to attend.'

'Then do so. If not with my blessing, at least with my knowledge. I'm glad you consulted me . . . Well, told me, anyway. When is the funeral?'

'Tomorrow afternoon.'

'It's not a cremation?'

'I don't think Mrs Ruding would go in for cremation. She'd want the full thing, a church service followed by a graveside ceremony. Not for religious reasons, but because funerals should be family occasions with all the proper trimmings.'

Rosa and Peter arrived at the church early and sat in a pew at the rear from where they could observe everything.

Rosa noticed that almost all the women were wearing black and most of the men had on black ties. She was glad she had decided to wear one of her more sombre outfits. She couldn't help reflecting, however, that at the last funeral she had attended, that of a sparky old aunt who had lived life to the full, the mourners were all colourfully dressed and there had been an atmosphere of scarcely suppressed exuberance. This was at the request of the deceased, who had wanted the nearest the Church of England could get to a New Orleans jazz-band-type funeral.

The pall bearers appeared at the west door of the church and began their slow journey down the aisle. The coffin was piled high with flowers, mostly expensive wreaths, but with one floral replica of a Formula One racing car. Rosa recalled that car racing had been one of Eddie's lifetime passions.

Behind the coffin came Mrs Ruding, her hair a fresh shade of orange-red and covered by a black gossamer scarf. Two tough-looking men supported her, one on either side. Rosa decided they were probably her brothers. Behind them came a phalanx of other relatives, the men stern-faced, the women dabbing their eyes.

'See anyone you recognise?' Peter whispered as the service began.

'Detective Chief Inspector Cain. And I've just spotted Joe Gillfroy at the far end of the pew behind us.'

'I wonder if Tam Grigg is here.'

'Joe may be able to tell us.'

'We can offer him a lift to the cemetery.'

Rosa nodded. She wondered how many of the congregation were there as observers rather than mourners. Was it possible that the small, anonymous-looking man two pews ahead belonged to MI5? Or perhaps the rather pretty girl wearing a black velvet beret came from that faceless department?

The service came to an end and the coffin was borne out to the waiting hearse. Rosa moved to cut off Joe's departure.

'Hello, Joe,' she said. 'Can we offer you a lift to the cemetery?'

'Good gracious, I never expected to see you here,' he exclaimed.

'Our car's just round the corner.'

Joe looked about him with quick darting glances before responding.

'If you're sure it's not putting you to any trouble.'

'None at all. By the way, this is a friend who has come with me. Peter Chen.'

The two men shook hands, Joe somewhat nervously. They got into Peter's BMW and moved off in the direction of the cemetery.

'Did you recognise many people in church?' Rosa asked, turning her head to speak to Joe in the back seat.

'They were mostly Mrs Ruding's family. She was the eldest of twelve and those were her brothers and sisters and their spouses all around her.'

'Was Tam Grigg there?'

Joe shook his head. 'He knows when not to show his face.'

'Chief Inspector Cain was in church,' Rosa said and watched Joe's expression.

'Where was he sitting?'

'On the opposite side to you and nearer the front. Has he tried to get in touch with you since your court appearance?'

Joe shrugged. 'I've changed my address.'

'I'm sure he'd like to have a talk to you.'

'Possibly, but I don't want to talk to him.'

'And yet you phoned him and suggested meeting him in St Anne's churchyard.'

'Things are different now, aren't they?' he said darkly. 'And as I'm now your client, etiquette prevents your telling the police anything about me.'

Shortly afterwards, they turned in through the cemetery gates and parked in a line of black limousines.

'Thanks for the ride,' Joe said and got out without waiting for Rosa or Peter.

'He seemed in a hurry to get out of our company,' Peter observed. 'He's foxy all right. I wouldn't trust him an inch.'

'I don't.'

They walked along a path which ran between two rows of graves. A huddle of mourners could be seen ahead, together with a priest, his white surplice ruffled by the breeze.

After a tortuous journey through life, Eddie had reached his final resting place. His mother and her relatives were grouped around the grave, the men looking sterner than ever, the women sobbing more openly. Only Mrs Ruding appeared to be resolutely composed as she stood watching her son's coffin being lowered into the ground.

Maybe, Rosa thought, she has done her crying. On the other hand she hadn't struck Rosa as someone easily given to tears.

As the service of committal continued to its lugubrious end, the family's emotions became noisier, orchestrated by a large, fat woman whom Rosa took to be one of Charlotte Ruding's sisters.

Rosa and Peter hung back and observed the scene from a slight distance. She noticed Chief Inspector Cain moving quietly amongst the mourners as if taking a roll-call. As for Joe, he seemed to have disappeared.

The service came to an end and Rosa was turning away when a man she had noticed standing apart from the family came toward her and Peter.

'Nothing like a funeral for bringing people together,' he remarked. 'Do you think it's all right to smoke now?'

Rosa realised he was addressing Peter rather than herself.

'I wondered if you'd be here,' he went on.

'This is Eddie's brother whom I met in Amsterdam last week,' Peter said and made the introduction.

'So you were Eddie's lawyer,' he said, giving Rosa an appraising look. 'I should think you're glad you don't have too many clients like him. If you take my advice, you'll steer clear of the Rudings.' He glanced around.

'I think I'll make my getaway. Don't want to tangle with any of the family.' Without further speech, he hurried off.

'If Vincent Ruding isn't on speaking terms with any of his relatives, how did he find out about the funeral?' Rosa said in a thoughtful voice as she and Peter got into the car to drive back into central London. 'Somebody must have been in touch with him about the arrangements.'

Chapter 12

Tam Grigg spent that same afternoon in his gymnasium. Later he was going to his cousin's home for a meeting with Alex and two others to discuss plans to burgle a safe-deposit vault where, with luck, the haul could be worth several million. One of the men worked there and knew all the security arrangements. He was a trusted employee at the moment, but was bound to come under suspicion after the operation. It was essential to ensure his silence when the police questioned him, hence Grigg had decided to take his girlfriend hostage and let the man know that a word out of turn would result in her death; followed by the man's own, though he'd not mentioned that small detail. The man was known to be besotted with his girlfriend, though Grigg felt totally unsentimental about their future.

The plan had been carefully prepared and D-day had been set. But now there was a fly in the ointment. A fly in the shape of Joe Gillfroy – or rather his arrest for loitering with intent in the vicinity of the jeweller's shop.

The police had been to the shop and asked a lot of questions. But they had learnt nothing from the man who managed it. What Grigg didn't know, however, was what Joe had told the police about the shop.

These were the thoughts that passed through his mind as he had his work-out in the gym. The grunts from his exertions seemed to take on a more menacing sound. By the time he reached the swimming pool, he had reluctantly decided the operation would have to be postponed. With luck, it need not be for long. But Joe Gillfroy was a two-faced little creep whom one couldn't trust. Sooner or later he would come to a bad end.

He climbed out of the pool and towelled himself vigorously. Then he went over to the wall telephone and dialled a number.

'That you, Alex?' he said when his cousin answered. 'I've been thinking . . .'

Alex listened in obedient silence until given an opportunity to speak.

'I don't like it either, Tam. What was the little runt doing there at two o'clock in the morning? You can bet it wasn't a coincidence that it was Olson's place.'

'And why wasn't I told earlier?'

'That was unfortunate, Tam, I have to admit. Olson didn't report it immediately because he was in a tizzy about his daughter giving birth that day. And because the premises weren't actually broken into, he didn't think it was particularly serious and dismissed it from his mind. I've now straightened out his thinking, Tam.'

'Good. You can remind him that he's not irreplaceable.'

'Shall be done. What is a bit worrying,' Alex went on, 'is that the police asked for a remand in order to make further enquiries.'

'What further enquiries?' Grigg asked sharply.

'That's what's worrying.'

'Do we know where to find Joe Gillfroy?' Grigg asked after a pause.

'He shifts around a bit, but I can probably find out.'

'Do that and let me know. I think he and I had better have a chat. A heart-to-heart,' he added in a grim tone.

* * *

79

Joe Gillfroy had a strong instinct for survival. He needed it. Running with the hare and hunting with the hounds called for considerable nimbleness.

Though people like Grigg regarded him as a duplicitous small crook, he was pleased to think that he maintained certain standards. He sought always to be courteous and took great trouble to speak what he was pleased to think was the Queen's English. He looked down on those who were branded as common criminals, whether they belonged in the big time or in a lower league. Despite his occasional brushes with the law, he certainly never thought of himself as a criminal. In his case it was simply misfortune. Fate delivering an indiscriminate slap.

What was currently occupying his mind was getting his hands on the reward for unmasking Eddie Ruding's murderer. He was sure there must be a reward. The police had a fund from which such payments were made. He knew that because he had benefited in the past, though he had never had more than the equivalent of a small win.

Joe had had no intention of attending Eddie's interment, but had not liked to say so when Rosa offered him a lift. Hence he had accepted the offer and later played hide-and-seek behind gravestones before making his escape and catching a bus home.

He had seen all he wanted to see at the church. Moreover, he had an aversion to cemeteries, preferring not to be reminded of his own mortality.

The next evening saw him at his favourite watering-hole. Although he changed his address with depressing regularity, he always returned to the same pub and never felt more at ease than when sitting in a corner of the saloon bar with a glass of malt whisky in his hand. When he couldn't afford whisky, he had half a pint of Guinness and when that, too, was beyond his pocket, he made do with a lemon shandy. The landlord, who was a benign man, often gave him a drink on the house, in return for which Joe would feed him items of gossip about certain of his customers.

On this particular evening he had just settled down in his usual corner with a large malt whisky when he became aware of someone standing over him.

'Evening, Joe,' Alex said when Joe looked up.

'Oh, hello. Haven't seen you here before.'

'That's right, but I heard I might find you here. There's somebody outside who'd like to have a word with you.'

Joe knew better than to ask who. Instead he said, 'How is Tam?'

'Looking forward to having a chat with you.'

'Have I time to finish my drink?'

'Yes, but don't take too long about it. The car's parked on a double yellow line.'

Joe quickly swallowed his drink and stood up. He caught the landlord's eye and gave him a resigned shrug and a flip of his hand as he followed Alex out of the pub.

Tam Grigg was sitting in his car about fifty yards along the street. He motioned Joe to join him in the back. At the wheel was a young man with a cropped head and a neck half the width of his shoulders. As soon as Alex got into the passenger seat, the car moved off.

'We'll just drive around and have a chat,' Grigg said.

'Anything you say,' Joe replied obligingly.

'It's come to my ears, Joe, that you've been telling people I was responsible for Eddie's death.' Joe shook his head vigorously. 'I hope it's not true,' Grigg went on, 'because I don't appreciate being slandered. Mind you, I didn't think it could be true, because, as I said to Alex, Joe's too wised up to try and involve me in something I had no part of.'

'That's right, Tam.'

'Good.' Grigg gazed out of the car window for a few moments before turning his attention back to Joe. 'What were you doing at Olson's the jeweller's the other night? Loitering with intent, I'm told.'

Joe gave an uncomfortable squirm. 'I was passing the end of the alleyway when I heard a noise. It sounded like a baby crying and I thought perhaps a child had been left there. Abandoned. I just went to investigate and was looking around when this young constable appeared. I had no idea I was at the rear of a jeweller's shop. Olson's, did you say?' He gave Grigg a sickly smile and turned to glance out of the window. 'Where are you taking me?' he asked anxiously.

'Not worried, are you?'

'What have I got to be worried about?'

'Exactly.'

'Well, if that's all you wanted to know, drop me off at a bus stop and I'll make my way home.'

'All in good time, Joe. All in good time.'

An oppressive silence filled the car. Then about fifteen minutes later it turned off the road on to a track and came to a stop in some trees.

'Where are we?' Joe asked in alarm.

'Hampstead Heath. I'd have thought you'd have recognised it.'

'I don't know this part of London,' Joe said through clenched teeth.

'It can be a scene of great activity on a summer's evening. Girls get raped and even murders take place without anyone being the wiser. That baby you heard outside Olson's would never attract attention up here. The poor little mite could cry its head off without being heard.'

Joe nervously licked his lips. 'If it suits you, I'll get out here and catch a bus.'

Ignoring the suggestion, Grigg went on, 'There's a pond the other side of those trees. When they dredged it recently, they found a man's body on the bottom. It was weighted with enough old iron to fill a scrapyard. The police reckoned he was a small-time operator who had grassed once too often.' He fixed Joe with a dispassionate stare. 'Makes you think a bit, doesn't it?'

Joe nodded, which was about the only thing he felt capable of doing. But Grigg hadn't yet finished with him.

'And now, because this is your lucky day, we'll drive you home. I'd like to see where you live, anyway.'

Twenty minutes later the car stopped outside a dingy terraced house near St Pancras station. Not for the first time in his life, Joe was scared. Even so, it was surprising how quickly his sense of survival asserted itself. He would visit his solicitor and tell her what had happened. Grigg's threats and insinuations were surely the clearest possible evidence of his involvement in Eddie's death.

He didn't believe that Grigg had killed him with his own hands; not nowadays when he could get others to do that sort of work for him. The driver of the car, for instance, who hadn't uttered a word throughout the evening. He looked capable of breaking someone's neck as easily as he might snap a dry twig.

Rosa was not at all pleased when she arrived at her office the next morning to find Joe Gillfroy on the doorstep.

'I did ask you to phone and make an appointment before coming,' she said somewhat crossly.

'Something happened yesterday evening which made it imperative that I came to see you without delay. It's nothing to do with my court appearance. Well, not directly.'

'Well, you can come in for fifteen minutes and then I have to go out.'

He followed her through the street door and up the stairs to Snaith and Epton's office where he received a chilly look from Stephanie.

'So what's happened?' Rosa enquired in a mildly exasperated tone when they reached her room.

Joe needed no second invitation to relate the events of the previous evening. It was a factual account, embellished only by the heroic light in which he cast his own behaviour.

'Do you want the police informed?' Rosa asked when he had finished. 'It's essentially a matter for them.'

'Perhaps later,' he said. 'But do you agree it all points to Grigg being Eddie's murderer?'

'Not conclusively.'

'But why should he have tried to frighten me off my own enquiries, if he's not guilty?'

'I think Grigg may regard you as a nuisance rather than a threat. I imagine from all I've heard about him that he's used to intimidating people. It's part of his armoury. He's obviously suspicious of what you were up to near Olson's shop in the small hours of the morning. Clearly he didn't believe the story you told him, and nor would anyone with a grain of intelligence, so you'd better think up something more plausible when we go to court next time.' She paused and studied the unappealing figure in her visitors' chair. She would have liked to tell him to have a good wash before he next came to her office, but that would have been unkind.

'I hope I wasn't followed when I came here this morning,' he said suddenly.

'Any reason to suppose you were?' Rosa asked in a startled voice.

'I feel Grigg will try and keep me under surveillance,' he replied.

Rosa decided this was, as likely as not, a flight of Joe's imagination. She couldn't believe that Tam Grigg didn't have better things to do than keep tabs on her rather pathetic client. That is, unless there were matters of which she was unaware. Such a possibility certainly existed.

Glancing at her watch, she said, 'I have to go or I'll be late at court. Make an appointment to come and see me early next week. We'll review the whole situation and discuss the loitering with intent charge.'

In her hurry to leave, she didn't notice a jeep-type Suzuki parked twenty yards along the street. It had special tinted glass so that she wouldn't in any event have observed the features of the person behind the steering-wheel.

He was a young man with cropped hair and a thick bull-like neck.

Chapter 13

'Flaming kids! I'll break their ruddy necks if I ever catch 'em.'

Sorely tried as he frequently was, this was the strongest language that Ted Jacomb ever used. The cause of his outburst on this occasion was the absence of his handcart from where he had left it the previous evening. The trouble was that though the cemetery gates were locked overnight, there were places in the perimeter fence where anybody could clamber through. Ted was always making complaints, but no one seemed interested in putting things right, each authority blaming another. Ted, who had become cemetery keeper after being invalided out of the army, would be glad when he could retire and shed his responsibilities. He was tired of fighting a losing battle against weeds and vandals and the inertia of the local council concerned.

But meanwhile where was his handcart?

His gaze roamed over the cemetery with its rows of hotchpotch tombstones. As an ex-military man, Ted was as much offended by them as by a parade of soldiers of differing height in a variety of uniforms. Whenever he had visited military cemeteries, he had always been impressed by the uniformity and simplicity of the graves.

He thought he could see his cart in the area where there were a number of new graves. As yet none of them had headstones or were more than elongated patches of freshly laid turf sprinkled with rapidly dying flowers. In Ted's view, they were better that way, but he knew that all too soon freshly engraved marble slabs would be erected with their often cloying inscriptions.

He reached his handcart and gave it a quick examination. At least it didn't appear to have been damaged or to be filled with flowers taken from surrounding graves, or, as on one occasion, to have a dead cat lying on the bottom.

He glanced around him and was about to wheel his cart

away when something caught his eye. It was the grave of the chap who had been murdered. It was still covered with flowers, long past their best. It looked, however, as if the racing car made of spring flowers and evergreen material, which crowned the grave, had been damaged.

'Ruddy vandals,' Ted muttered to himself. 'Don't they have any respect, even for the dead?'

He stepped across the intervening graves to see what had happened. At first he thought it was the branch of a tree that had been thrown down, with a couple of wreaths lying on top. Then as his gaze shifted he noticed a man's head sticking out. He suddenly realised that he was staring down at a man's body lying on top of the grave with a scattering of flowers over him. The now somewhat battered racing car covered most of his head and shoulders and there was a wreath across the small of his back and another over his lower legs.

Ted had, on occasions, found vagrants asleep in the cemetery, but never on top of a grave. This, however, was a body that had been brought there and deliberately left where it now lay. He realised with revulsion the use to which his handcart had been put.

'Ruddy hell,' he murmured, as he turned and hurried off to the small office which was attached to the chapel of rest.

From there he phoned the police. Fortunately the cemetery was deserted at that hour, though there was to be a funeral later in the day. But actual visitors were relatively few, just one or two regulars who liked the tranquillity of a cemetery and came to contemplate.

About twenty minutes later he saw a police car pull up at the main gate and two uniformed officers walked over to where he was standing. One of them, a sergeant, bent down and gingerly lifted the dead man's head.

'Can't see any sign of injury,' he remarked. 'Wonder what he died of?'

'Maybe he was trying to save on funeral expenses,' his colleague observed.

86

'I don't want any of your mortuary humour,' the sergeant said sternly.

As he spoke, he reached carefully into the dead man's jacket pocket and pulled out a piece of paper.

'Who's Rosa Epton when she's at home?' he said, holding the piece of paper out for his companion to see.

'Never heard of her. Presumably that's her phone number beside the name.'

Half an hour later Rosa received a call from the police. After listening to what they had to say, she told them that the man described sounded like a client of hers named Joe Gillfroy. When she added that, as far as she knew, he lived alone and had no close family, she was asked if she would come and identify the body, and agreed.

Before leaving, she called Detective Chief Inspector Cain and told him what had happened. He thanked her and said he would meet her at the cemetery.

When Rosa arrived she found a police officer on guard at the entrance and the public being refused admission. After declaring her credentials, however, she was allowed in. She could see people moving about in the vicinity of Eddie's grave, which was screened off. Cain met her as she reached the area and led her behind the screen.

'Yes, that's Joe Gillfroy,' she said with a small shiver.

His body was lying on a stretcher waiting to be removed to the mortuary. The swarm of experts who descend instantly on the scene of a murder were doing what was required of them. Some, like the photographer, had already departed, others on hands and knees were sifting through debris.

'Has the cause of death yet been established?' Rosa asked as she turned away from the body.

'First indications', Cain said, 'are that he died of a broken neck, same as Eddie Ruding.'

'So you saw Gillfroy as recently as yesterday morning?' Cain said as he and Rosa sat in an office at the local police station.

He had explained his interest to the divisional detective superintendent who was nominally in charge of the investigation.

Rosa nodded. 'He was waiting outside my office when I arrived. I wasn't very pleased to see him and said I was shortly going to court, but that he could come in.'

'And he told you how Grigg had threatened him the previous evening? If he's to be believed, it was a determined attempt to scare him off. The only thing that surprises me is that Grigg wasted time doing that. If he thought he was being grassed on, I'd have expected him to have given Gillfroy the chop there and then. He's not the sort of man to give people second chances.'

'He must have had a reason for acting as he did.'

'Yes, but what?'

'Perhaps he wasn't absolutely satisfied what Joe was up to.'

'I don't think the likes of Grigg feel they must be satisfied beyond a reasonable doubt before they act,' Cain observed in a wry tone.

'What I meant was that Joe was more valuable to him alive than dead.'

'It didn't stay that way for long.'

'Not if one assumes Grigg is the murderer.'

Cain gave her a surprised look, 'You mean, you don't think he is?'

'I don't know. If I accept everything Joe told me, I agree that Grigg is your man. But I never felt that Joe was telling me the whole truth. Rather that I was being given a well-tailored account to suit his own purposes.'

Cain sighed. 'One thing for sure, Grigg must be further interviewed. It'll be interesting to hear what he has to say about the expedition to Hampstead Heath.'

'If he denies it took place, there's no other evidence now that Joe is dead.'

'I don't give up as easily as that. If he does deny that he ever met Joe that evening and I can catch him out in a single lie, he'd better watch his step. With luck I'll find somebody who saw Joe leaving the pub with Grigg's cousin. Even somebody who saw the car parked on the Heath.' He paused. 'If Grigg has any sense – and that's what I'm afraid of – he'll admit most of the facts, but deny the intimidation, and, of course, deny any involvement in Joe's death. And I've got to talk to Mrs Ruding even if she doesn't want to talk to me.' He gave Rosa an irritated look. 'It's a pity Joe didn't keep his rendezvous with me. If he had, he might still be alive. Ditto if you'd informed me immediately of his visit to you.'

Rosa was about to make an indignant retort, but refrained. She wanted to keep in with Cain and not alienate him. But she never enjoyed being reproached. First her partner and now the police.

'Well, I'd best be getting back to my office,' she said. 'I've done all that was required of me, namely identified the dead man.'

'Yes. And thank you for coming, Miss Epton. I expect I'll be in touch again before long.' He gave her a sardonic smile. 'Let's hope no more of your clients end up with broken necks.'

As she drove back, she reflected on Cain's parting words. There was something particularly cruel and nasty about the two murders. The perpetrator had to be someone with a thoroughly warped mind.

Chapter 14

Later that day Dr Felling carried out a post mortem examination and confirmed when speaking to Cain on the phone that Joe had died from an identical type of blow to the neck as that sustained by Eddie Ruding, except in his case it had not needed to be so severe. He had also discovered that

Joe was suffering from cancer of the stomach and hadn't had long to live, though this condition had played no part in his death.

'Mustn't he have been having treatment?' Cain asked, hoping to be given a further line of enquiry.

'It was in a relatively early stage. He probably thought it was indigestion and sucked a lozenge he bought at the chemist. By the time he went to see a doctor, it would have been too late. It was obvious he didn't look after himself from a dietary point of view. Most likely he smoked and drank too much and lived on junk food, greasy chips covered with vinegar. A spell in prison might have saved him. A regular regime, wholesome food and proper medical attention.'

'The prison service could use you as their public relations officer,' Cain remarked with a laugh. 'As a matter of fact I've found out only this afternoon that Gillfroy had served one short term in prison. Six weeks for indecent exposure. He had other convictions for the same offence, but managed to avoid being put inside.'

'Poor chap!' Dr Felling remarked with a sad shake of his head. 'Doesn't sound as if he had much of a life, though maybe he had his moments of pleasure.'

'Like exposing himself on Wimbledon Common.'

'That wasn't what I meant,' the pathologist said reprovingly.

He had just finished speaking on the phone to Dr Felling when Detective Sergeant Saddler came in.

'Yes, Chris, any news?'

'Tam Grigg seems to have disappeared.'

'What do you mean by disappeared?'

'He's not at home and nobody knows where he is. At least, they probably know, but they're not telling.'

'When was he last seen?'

'This morning. Packed a small bag and departed.'

'How did you find this out?'

'I picked up the young thug who calls himself his chauffeur. He said he'd driven Grigg to Gatwick and left him

90

there. He professed to having no idea where he was going or for how long.'

'What about Grigg's cousin, Alex Cartwright?'

'He's also temporarily missing.'

'If Grigg doesn't reappear within a few days, we'll alert Interpol. Meanwhile we must try and find out how Gillfroy spent his last few hours. He visited Rosa Epton's office around nine yesterday morning. Where'd he go after that?'

Saddler gave his chief inspector an impassive glance and departed. He reckoned life would become easier when Mrs Cain had given birth. He himself had first become a father at the age of twenty-two. Leaving it until you were nearly forty was like going on a roller-coaster after a heavy meal. Exciting but hazardous.

When he arrived at the airport that afternoon, Vincent Ruding was alarmed to find the whole place swarming with policemen. Wherever he looked, there seemed to be uniformed officers of both sexes, standing and observing, with the gateways to Customs and Immigration under particular surveillance.

He thrust his way to the check-in desk for his flight to Amsterdam. In as casual a voice as possible he asked the girl on duty why the police were there in such strength.

'They're expecting trouble from soccer fans who are on their way back from Portugal. I gather their side lost so they may vent their feelings on our fixtures when they arrive.'

Ruding let out a quiet sigh of relief and returned her smile. 'Seems they play soccer all the year round nowadays.'

'As far as I'm concerned they can play in the Colosseum in Rome, I'm still not interested,' she said, as she glanced past him at the next passenger in line.

He approached passport control with new-found nonchalance. Nevertheless, it had given him a bit of a fright seeing the law out in such force.

91

He had stayed on a few days after his brother's funeral, but was now looking forward to getting back to Holland, which he regarded as home. While in England he had made no attempt to get in touch with his mother. He wasn't even sure if she'd seen him at the church or later at the cemetery. Not that that bothered him. He hadn't come over to make peace with his mother. Indeed, paying his last respects to his dead brother hadn't been the main purpose of his visit.

He had phoned Colin Kirby on a number Eddie had given him and they had met at a pub near Victoria station on the evening of the funeral. But Kirby had been in a guarded mood and made it clear he had only agreed to meet him out of professional duty. He had particularly wanted to know whom Eddie had met during his visit to Amsterdam. But if Kirby had been uncommunicative, so had Vincent. It had been an unsatisfactory meeting all round and Kirby had got up and left after a single round of drinks.

Later that same evening in a different pub he had met Joe Gillfroy. He didn't know Joe well and didn't like him. Moreover, he didn't trust him, even if on occasions he had used him on Eddie's recommendation. He had certainly been a useful link since Eddie's death. On this occasion he had talked mysteriously about how crafty he was and how poor old Joe would yet be rich old Joe. Vincent had considered it dangerous talk and said so. And now Joe was neither poor nor rich, but dead.

Vincent had much on his mind as his plane headed across the North Sea and he found his spirits quietly sinking before it even touched down at Schipol airport. His arrival home did nothing to revive them. The parrot gave him a surly look and his wife informed him that 'that man' had been in touch again.

'What man?' he asked testily, knowing full well.

'The one your brother stole money from,' she replied and continued to stare at him until he walked out of the room.

Chapter 15

'What we have to do is go back to the beginning,' Peter said.

'Which beginning?' Rosa asked. 'There've been several.'

'The tram incident in Amsterdam. Or rather your spotting Eddie in the café on Leidseplein.'

They were sitting in a small Chelsea restaurant which had excellent food, with matching prices.

But as Peter had said when he picked her up at her flat, 'We deserve a slap-up dinner tonight. At least, you do.'

It was the day on which Rosa had been asked to identify Joe's body. To her the day had seemed endless and it was a relief to be sitting in civilised surroundings with a delicious dinner in prospect. Under the influence of a second Bloody Mary she was slowly relaxing. She never touched alcohol until the working day was over and savoured it the more for that.

She ordered the same as she had on their last two occasions at the restaurant, namely a pancake filled with spinach and covered with a cheese sauce followed by scampi meunière in a circle of fluffy rice.

'I'm sure that everything that's happened relates back to Amsterdam,' Peter continued. 'Why were Eddie and his companions so upset at being seen?'

'You tell me.'

'At first I was sure it was because Eddie was on the run from prison, but that theory collapsed when we learnt he had been released by the powers that be. So what was it he didn't want you to report on? The answer has to lie with the identities of his companions.'

'But I'd never seen either of them in my life,' Rosa said.

'I know. That wouldn't prevent them, however, being worried about your reaction. If you'd reported the incident, I'm sure that MI5, for example, would have asked you for descriptions of the two men.'

'Which I wouldn't have been able to provide. At least, not descriptions of any value.'

'They weren't to know that. You might have been quietly observing them for several minutes. They obviously kept us under surveillance and engineered the tram incident on our way back to the hotel after dinner. It could easily have succeeded.'

Rosa shivered. 'But who was the boy on the bicycle?'

'Somebody paid to cause an accident. If he'd been caught, he only had to say that it was an accident. Everyone knows that cyclists and pedestrians and trams dice with death in Amsterdam.'

'If you're right,' Rosa said in a thoughtful voice, 'it could mean that the two men we saw with Eddie tie in with the burglary of Bilak's flat.'

'For all we know, one of them might have been Bilak. He could have established a new base in Holland and kept tabs on Eddie. As soon as he was released from prison, a trap was baited to get him to Amsterdam.'

'I can't see Eddie walking into a trap as easily as that.'

'We don't know what the bait was.'

'He didn't appear to be under any sort of restraint when we saw him drinking at the café.'

'True. So perhaps he didn't need much luring.'

'I suppose it may have been an attempt to get Eddie to work for the opposition.'

'It's a possibility. They'd have had a hold over him. There was the six thousand pounds he'd nicked.'

'But he'd been sentenced for that, so it couldn't have been used to put pressure on him.'

At that moment, the waiter brought their first course and Rosa banished Eddie Ruding and Amsterdam temporarily from her mind. Peter, however, looked preoccupied as he scooped out a piece of melon.

'I take your point,' he said, after a pause during which Rosa had concentrated on eating. 'But intelligence services are adept at twisting people's tails, particularly people like

94

Eddie who frequently live outside the law. Incidentally, did he ever tell you how much he was being paid to break into Bilak's flat?'

'He got a hundred pounds on account, with two hundred more to come on successful conclusion of the operation.'

'That doesn't sound very generous.'

Rosa shrugged. 'It's taxpayers' money. They can't throw it around like an oil sheik's. And anyway he collected six thousand.'

'Plus five years in jail.'

Rosa sat back with a contented sigh. 'That pancake was delicious. There were times when I thought the day would never come to an end. Now I don't mind if it doesn't.'

Peter gave her a faint leer. 'I can think of the best place to end it.'

Rosa smiled happily and turned her attention to the plate of scampi that had just been placed in front of her.

For a while they ate in silence, then Rosa said, 'I wonder what part Vincent Ruding has in all this?'

'A larger one, I suspect, than he has let on.'

'I suppose he could even have murdered his brother.'

'That applies to almost everyone, save the man in the moon. As far as we know, however, Vincent didn't have a motive.'

Rosa put down her knife and fork and looked thoughtful. 'I recall Joe saying that Eddie appeared, in his own words, to have got himself a nice little meal ticket.'

'Meaning?'

'A regular supply of easy money. And in Eddie's language, that could mean only one thing. The question is, whom was he blackmailing? Joe thought it was Grigg, but I wonder . . .'

'It's Mrs Charlotte Ruding speaking,' said the familiar voice when Stephanie put through the call soon after Rosa had reached her office the next morning. Rosa reflected it was odd that the telephone should bring out such primness in somebody who was anything but prim in face-to-face conversation. Presumably she was one of those people who viewed the telephone with suspicion and hostility. 'I'm ringing to see 'ow you're getting on,' she continued, adding, 'getting on with investigating my Eddie's death. I 'eard yesterday that Grigg 'as disappeared. That shows 'e done it.'

'I did tell you, Mrs Ruding, that there was very little I'd be able to do,' Rosa said patiently.

'If it's more money you want, you've only to say so.'

'It has nothing to do with money. It's a question of resources. I'm a lawyer, not a private eye.'

'What resources does a private eye 'ave that you 'aven't got?'

'Plenty,' Rosa said firmly and went on quickly, 'I don't suppose you saw me, but I came to Eddie's funeral.'

'I saw you. You were with a Chinese chap.'

'He's a solicitor friend. I gather your other son came over from Holland.'

'So I 'eard. Don't know why 'e bothered to come. Or 'ow 'e found out when it was.'

'My guess would be that Joe Gillfroy informed him.'

'That little snake! You 'eard what 'e went and done afterwards? Disgraceful I call it. I'm writing to the council to tell 'em what I think. Things like that shouldn't be allowed to 'appen. I paid for Eddie's grave and 'e's entitled to be left in peace, not 'ave other people's bodies dropped on top of 'im.'

Rosa decided that silence would be her wisest comment on Mrs Ruding's denunciation of the council and the unfortunate Joe.

'It looks very much as if the same person killed both your son and Gillfroy,' she said after a pause. 'I'm sure the police are working on that theory.'

'All they've got to do is find Grigg.'

'I've told Chief Inspector Cain that you're certain Grigg is the murderer and I've no doubt they'll give him a tough interrogation when he turns up.' Ignoring the contemptuous snort that came down the line, she went on, 'I'll certainly pass on to you anything I hear, though it seems your sources of information are better than mine.'

'So you've changed your mind about 'elping my Eddie. I thought 'is memory meant something to you. 'E 'ad faith in you. Said to come to you if I 'ad any problems.'

Rosa let out a silent sigh. To be reproached, then shamelessly cajoled by this hennaed old woman was more than she deserved. She was about to defend herself when Mrs Ruding got in first.

'I assure you my money's as good as anyone's.'

'It's nothing to do with money,' Rosa said in a tone of considerable exasperation, only to discover she was talking on a dead line.

Of all the maddening women, she reflected, Mrs Ruding must be a candidate for a gold medal.

She was still fuming and trying to rationalise Mrs Ruding's conduct when there was a knock on her door and Ben came in.

'Morning, Miss E,' he said in his usual cheerful way. 'This has just come. Got held up because it didn't have enough stamps on it.' As he spoke he put down on Rosa's desk a small package which gave the appearance of having had a lifetime of travel. The wrapping paper was creased and sealed with two pieces of sticky paper, one at either end. Rosa looked at it with suspicion. 'It's all right, Miss E, it's not a bomb,' Ben went on. 'At least it's not ticking and it doesn't have any smell.'

'What do you think it is, Ben?' Rosa said.

'From its size and shape, I'd say it could be a wristwatch or one of those pen and pencil sets people get at Christmas and give away the next one.'

'Is there a postmark?'

'Can't read it. It's just a black smear.' Ben held it up to his ear and gave it a good shake while Rosa observed him with tolerant amusement. Whatever the contents, they didn't seem ready to blow up. 'Like me to open it, Miss E?'

97

'Yes, but still take care, Ben,' Rosa said after a moment of thought. She didn't seriously believe it was another attempt on her life, but . . .

'I'll hold it behind the curtain to be on the safe side.'

Rosa watched as Ben unwrapped the package, shielded by the heavy curtain at her window. It was like handling radioactive material from a safe distance, she thought.

Suddenly something fell to the ground and Ben stooped to pick it up.

'It's a key,' he announced. 'And there's another. Also a letter.'

He returned to Rosa's desk and placed a doorkey on it. He then shook a further key from the package and handed her a heavily folded sheet of paper, which she spread out in front of her.

Memo to Miss Epton from Mr Gillfroy, she read. Beneath this formal opening it continued:

Herewith keys to my current abode, the smaller one is the key to my room on the ground floor. I am sending them to you for use should anything happen to me. I'm almost sure I was followed when I left your office this morning. I decided to get further keys cut immediately as a precaution and send one set to you. Should it be necessary, please deal with my few belongings as you see fit. I haven't made a will because I don't have anyone to leave anything to. I'm afraid my life has been a steady descent. Well, some go up and some come down. All being well I'll be in touch with you shortly after you receive this and next time we meet I hope to be able to tell you more about Eddie's death. My address is 16 Conna Street, NW1.

Aware that Ben was observing her, Rosa said, 'They're keys to where Joe Gillfroy was living. I'm not really sure what to do.'

'Does he want you to take care of his affairs?' Ben asked.

'Such as they are, yes. Quite frankly, I wish this package had never arrived.'

'But it has, Miss E. Tell you what, why don't we go round there and take a look?' When Rosa assumed a dubious expression, he went on, 'He wouldn't have sent you his keys if he didn't want you to use them. He's relying on you, Miss E.'

Ben was never happier than when he and Rosa took off together on a bit of sleuthing. And it had to be said that he was an excellent companion and escort on such occasions.

Rosa glanced at the two keys and at Joe's memo. One way and another she felt he had been part of her life for much longer than he had. Though without any obvious charm, he had managed to enlist her interest, even sympathy, in his predicament. She recalled the first time they had met and the huge quantity of tea he had drunk.

'Are you doing anything this evening, Ben?' she asked, glancing up from her desk.

'Nothing that can't be rearranged,' he said quickly.

'You're not meeting . . . Clare?' For a moment she had not remembered the name of Ben's current girlfriend, who was relatively new in a longish line.

'Not till later,' he said. 'I'll let her know I'll probably be a bit late.'

'Then we'll set off around five thirty.'

She was grateful that Robin was taking a couple of days off as she would have felt obliged to tell him what she was proposing to do and would almost certainly have faced something less than enthusiasm. Peter was tied up with a client who had flown in from a tax-free haven, and was thus also out of reach. On balance, however, she was pleased to have Ben's support. He had the advantage of responding more flexibly to a situation than either Peter or Robin.

Conna Street turned out to be a cul-de-sac about half a mile north of St Pancras station. It had a single row of terraced houses on one side and a warehouse on the other. At the blind end there was a goods yard shut off by heavy wooden gates which were closed when Rosa and Ben arrived.

'There's number sixteen,' he said, pointing out of the window.

'I'll turn the car round at the end, so that we're pointing the right way when we leave.'

'Good idea,' Ben said, displaying the eagerness of a gun dog with the scent of a grouse moor in its nostrils.

Having turned the car round, Rosa parked a few doors from number sixteen and they got out.

'Give me the keys, Miss E,' Ben said as they reached the front door.

'I think we ought to ring the bell first. We'll only use the key if there's no reply.'

Ben nodded and gave the bell push a vigorous prod, followed by another a few seconds later.

The door opened abruptly to reveal an exceedingly fat man. He had a round, jowly face and a pair of darting, suspicious eyes.

'Yes?' he said.

'I believe Joe Gillfroy lodged here until recently,' Rosa said. 'I'm his solicitor.'

His eyes reflected a sudden beady interest. 'Come to settle his debts, have you? He owes a week's rent in advance for leaving without notice.'

'Come off it, mate,' Ben said. 'He was murdered, so how could he have given you notice?'

'Tough, but those are my rules. Anyway, why are you here?'

'I'd like to look round his room,' Rosa said in a mollifying tone. 'Can we come in?'

'You won't find nothing there. I've moved what there was. Can't afford to keep a room empty when it could be earning rent.'

'Where are his things now?'

'In a cupboard under the stairs. Just a couple of suitcases. I packed everything up after the police had gone.'

'When were they here?'

'Yesterday.'

'Did they go through his belongings?'

'Suppose so. I was in the kitchen answering their bleeding questions.'

'How many officers came?'

'Three. Three too many.'

'When did you first know Joe Gillfroy was dead?'

'When the police told me. Came as a bit of a shock. I don't like being mixed up with the police. There's enough aggro in life without *them.*'

Rosa contemplated the figure filling the doorway, who showed no inclination to let them in.

'If you let me know how much Gillfroy owed you, I'll arrange payment,' she said. 'And I'll remove his belongings out of your way. So may we come in?'

'All right. He owes me thirty pounds, if you'd like to give me that now.'

Rosa thought the sum had been plucked out of the air, but wasn't disposed to argue.

'Did Joe ever have visitors?' she asked, as she stepped into the dingy hall.

'No, unless you count the one who came the night he was killed. At the time I thought it was Joe himself coming in late. It was around three o'clock and I had a bad dose of indigestion and couldn't get to sleep. I heard the street door open and a minute later the door of Joe's room. I very nearly went down, just for a bit of company, but I didn't. Soon afterwards I must have fallen asleep. I got up around six thirty and went downstairs to make a cup of tea. I knocked on Joe's door to see if he'd like one too and when I didn't get a reply, I used my pass key. The room was empty. I assumed Joe had got up early and gone out. He did sometimes.'

'Had his bed been slept in?'

'Couldn't tell. It looked the same either way.'

'When did you last see Joe?'

'The previous afternoon. He went out around six and I never saw him again.'

'But you're certain you heard somebody enter the house and go into his room around three o'clock the next morning?'

'Yes.'

'Did you tell the police?'

'No, why should I?' he said defiantly. 'They'd still be here poking around if I'd told them. All I wanted was to get rid of them. There's no law that says you have to tell them everything. And, anyway, it could have been Joe himself coming in.'

Rosa pondered the possibility, but thought it unlikely. Much more probable was that the intruder was Joe's murderer and that Joe was dead by then. If that were so, it followed that the murderer had come looking for something specific or had wished to make sure there was nothing to incriminate him amongst Joe's pitiable belongings.

'I was about to have a bite to eat, so if that's all . . .'

'May we have a quick look round Joe's room?'

'I've told you, I've shifted his things out.'

'Nevertheless, I'd like to see inside.'

The man turned and opened a door on the right-hand side of the hall.

'This was his room. My best.'

Rosa and Ben stepped inside. It was the downstairs front room, austerely furnished and with a stale smell Rosa didn't try to analyse. A narrow bed, with a pile of blankets heaped at one end, ran the length of the wall behind the door. There was a rickety card table in the window with a forlorn-looking plant standing on it. Against the opposite wall was a varnished cupboard leaning at a precarious angle. Its handle had been replaced by a piece of coathanger and Rosa walked over and opened its door. It was empty apart from some old newspapers.

'I've told you I've moved all his stuff,' the man said irritably from the doorway.

'All right, we're going now,' Rosa said quickly to head off further argument. 'If you'll let me have the suitcases.'

'What about the money?'

'How much did you say?'

'Forty pounds.'

'Seems to have gone up.'

'Don't know what you mean.'

'You originally said thirty pounds.'

'That's right, Miss E,' Ben chimed in.

'You must have misheard. It's forty.'

Rosa was prepared to give him forty, as long as he didn't think she had not noticed the crude rip-off.

A few minutes later they departed, Ben carrying two battered suitcases which he put in the back of the car.

'I'd sooner live in a cardboard box than a room like that,' he said as they drove off.

'Certainly the air would be fresher.'

'Where are we going now, Miss E?'

'I'd like to take the suitcases back to the office.'

'Fine. Won't take us long to sort through the contents.'

'But I don't want to keep you from Clare.'

'That's all right. She won't mind. Anyway it's only seven o'clock. I'll buzz her when we get back to the office and say I've been held up on business.'

Ben had come a long way, Rosa reflected, since the day she had defended him on a housebreaking charge. After serving a sentence of youth custody he had arrived at Snaith and Epton's door seeking a job. Very few defendants, in her experience, heeded the somewhat sanctimonious admonition, beloved of judges, to become 'good citizens', but Ben was an honourable exception.

She was grateful to accept his offer to help unpack the suitcases. They probably contained nothing more than well-worn clothes. There certainly wouldn't be any valuables. His fat landlord would have seen to that in the unlikely event of there having been any. Nevertheless, she hoped the contents might reveal some clue to Joe's death.

It wouldn't be anything obvious for that would have been spotted by the police and removed.

It was easy to park at this hour of the evening and Rosa drew up immediately outside Snaith and Epton's street door. Together they mounted the stairs to the now deserted office and to Rosa's room.

'I noticed you didn't tell fatty we had keys to his house,' Ben remarked.

'I thought it better not to.'

Ben grinned. 'Let's hope these cases tell us why he sent you the keys.' He lay them side by side on the floor and knelt down in front. 'Which first, Miss E?'

'Whichever you like.'

'This one then, it's heavier than its mate.' As he pulled back the catches, the lid sprang up. 'One pair of shoes in need of repair,' he called out. 'One pair of smelly socks. Another pair of smelly socks. Two shirts, a towel, a woollen vest . . .' At this point he dug both hands into the case and rummaged around like a zealous customs officer. 'There's only clothes in this one, Miss E. Let's see what the other has to offer.'

'Hang on a moment, Ben. Isn't that a jacket at the bottom? Pull it out and see if there's anything in the pockets.'

'Yeah, there could be,' he remarked as he extracted the jacket and began deftly exploring its pockets.

'This of any interest?' he enquired, handing her a folded piece of paper which came from the inside wallet-pocket.

Rosa took it and studied it with a hopeful expression. It was a list showing sums of money against various dates. The amounts ranged from £25 to £100. The dates were all recent.

'Looks like he was a betting man,' Ben remarked.

'You think these represent winnings?' Rosa said.

'Or losses.'

'I suppose he could have been a gambler,' Rosa said doubtfully, 'but somehow I don't think so.' For a while she continued to stare thoughtfully at the piece of paper in her hand.

Meanwhile, Ben had knelt down in front of the second case and was fiddling with the catches. He lifted the top to reveal an assortment of articles. There were coathangers, talcum powder, shaving tackle, a pair of ancient bedroom slippers, a cheap alarm clock and two non-matching gloves. There was nothing of any documentary interest and Rosa concluded that whatever there might have been had been removed by the police. She sighed, for it was documents that were most likely to have provided clues to Joe's demise.

She decided she would call Cain the next day and ask him what the police had discovered. After all, she was still Joe's solicitor.

Ben stood up and dusted his knees. 'Shall I put it all away again, Miss E?'

'Just shove it back in. Then you'd better run off and keep your date with Clare.'

While Ben was tidying up, Rosa turned her attention back to the piece of paper she still held in her hand, wondering if it had any significance. As she stared at the dates with their corresponding sums of money, she suddenly spotted something she had previously missed.

All the dates were since Eddie Ruding's death.

Chapter 16

Tam Grigg paced restlessly up and down the veranda waiting for the telephone to ring. Alex normally called on the dot of nine o'clock every morning (French time), as instructed, but it was now twenty minutes after and the telephone remained silent. For the second time, Tam lifted the receiver to assure himself it was working properly.

The small villa where he was staying was on the southern

shore of Lake Geneva, a few miles out of Evian. Two-thirds of the lake's shoreline was in Switzerland, but this stretch was French. He had bought the villa a few years earlier and used it as a retreat.

Not for Tam Grigg – or Arnold Berger as his other passport declared him to be – a villa on the Costa del Sol in Spain. He preferred the lake, the mountains and the spaciousness of France to the high-rise apartment blocks along Spain's heavily populated Mediterranean coast. He could swim in the lake and drive up into the mountains to walk without being surrounded by other people. He appreciated solitude and enjoyed natural beauty, neither of which qualities made him any the less ruthless when it came to executing a robbery.

At last the phone rang and he leapt to answer it.

'Tam, it's me, Alex.'

'What the hell's kept you? You're half an hour late.'

'I know. I'm sorry, but it couldn't be helped.'

'What happened?'

'It was Shirley. She wanted me to take the cat to the vet. It's been very poorly.'

'Look, Alex, don't ever let that flaming cat come before me.' Grigg not only didn't like cats, he didn't like his cousin's wife either.

'It was the only time the vet could see her, Tam.'

'You and Shirley are both besotted with that animal,' Grigg observed sourly. 'Anyway, what's the latest news and I don't mean about the cat?'

'The police are still looking for you. We had a sergeant round again yesterday asking if I'd heard from you and did I know if you had a hide-out abroad?'

'You're not phoning from home now, are you?'

'Of course not. I'm at Shirley's sister's place. They're away, so it's safe to call from here. If the police have put a tap on my phone, they're welcome to listen to Shirley gossiping with her friends.'

'Shirley doesn't know my whereabouts, does she?'

106

'No. I've told her you're having a bit of a break in Majorca, but to keep it to herself.'

Tam grunted. 'Anything in today's papers about how police enquiries are going?'

'Not a word. You know how it is with the press, they lose interest as quickly as they show it.'

'Nothing to suggest they suspect me?'

'No . . . though your disappearance hasn't helped.'

Grigg frowned. Alex sounded a mite too complacent. If it were not for him, his cousin would be nobody. He certainly wouldn't be the owner of a nice home and an expensive car. Nor would he have an attractive blonde wife, though he would probably be better off without her and her flaming cat.

Alex went on, 'I called at Joe's address yesterday evening. The police had been there, but it didn't seem they'd found anything to help them. Also Joe's solicitor, Rosa Epton, had visited and collected all his stuff a few hours before I arrived.'

'She's a proper busybody,' Grigg observed in a musing tone. 'It was to her that Joe made a beeline after our little session with him on Hampstead Heath.'

'That's right, Tam.'

'Is Cliff still certain he wasn't spotted when he parked near her office that morning?'

'Yes.'

'Because if anyone put two and two together, or in this case, Cliff and Joe together, it could be awkward.'

'Don't worry, Tam, I'll keep my eyes and ears open.'

'What we need to do is provide the police with another line of enquiry. Sow a false trail, something of that sort.' After a pause he added, 'Call me this evening at six and I may have a few ideas. And Alex . . .'

'Yes, Tam?'

'Make sure it is six, even if the bleeding cat is at death's door.'

* * *

107

Cain was confident that, sooner or later, Tam Grigg would reappear. He hoped, of course, that it would be sooner. Interpol had circulated his particulars to all its members and Cain was optimistic that he would be tracked down before too long. Locating him, however, was only a first step. Interviewing him would be the second and possibly more difficult stage, depending on where he surfaced. These days criminals were as conversant with the ins and outs of extradition as lawyers.

Meanwhile, Cain glanced at the items laid on his desk which Sergeant Saddler had brought back from his search of Joe Gillfroy's room. There was a wad of correspondence reflecting a running battle between Joe and the Department of Social Security over the benefits to which he was entitled – or not entitled, as seemed more often to be the case. It showed that Joe was nothing if not persistent, with the department generally resistant to his claims.

There was a small grubby notebook which took Cain's attention. It contained seemingly meaningless jottings which probably had no bearing on his death, but which Cain knew he must try and make sense of. There were several telephone numbers which Sergeant Saddler was seeking to identify. Cain was not particularly hopeful that any of them would prove significant, but elimination formed a major part of any murder investigation.

There was a knock on his door and Saddler came in.

'Those phone numbers, sir,' he said, nodding in the direction of the notebook which lay open on Cain's desk. 'I've tracked them all down. The only interesting one is the eight three four number.'

'That's the Victoria area,' Cain broke in.

'Correct, sir. And the number in question is Colin Kirby's. He has a flat near the Tate Gallery.'

Cain frowned. 'Don't say that Gillfroy was another of Kirby's freelance troupe?'

'I suggest we visit him and find out. Shall I give him a buzz now?'

'He won't be there. He'll be at the office. Or should be by now.'

'No harm in trying the number, sir.'

Cain picked up his phone and dialled the number. 'His answering machine is on,' he said, a few seconds later. 'I'll see if he's in his office.'

But he wasn't and Cain found himself put through to John Decker.

'Good morning, Chief Inspector, is there something I can do to help?'

'I didn't mean to bother you,' Cain replied. 'I wasn't aware that you were fielding Kirby's calls.'

'I'm not, but when I was told you were on the line, I thought I might be able to assist.'

'I'd like to have a word with Kirby sometime. Do you know when he'll be around?'

'He'll be out most of the day, but he should be back in the office tomorrow. Shall I get a message to him?'

Cain hesitated. 'No, don't worry. I'll speak to him to-morrow.'

'You wouldn't like me to have him call you?'

'No. I'm going out shortly myself and am not sure when I'll be back.'

'Has something fresh come up?' Decker asked. He paused. 'Something I ought to know about?'

'No, nothing like that. I just wanted to clear up one or two small points from an earlier interview. Nothing that can't wait.' Following which he rang off as quickly as he could.

He didn't blame Decker for his blatant curiosity. It was perfectly natural in the circumstances, even if he, Cain, wasn't disposed to enlighten him. It was not that he didn't trust Decker, but MI5 was as capable as any other body of closing its ranks when one of its members was threatened from without. The police themselves were renowned for it. The time might come when he would need their close co-operation, but, for the moment, all he wanted to do was ask Kirby why someone as unlikely as Joe Gillfroy should have his home telephone number.

'I think we might pay him an unannounced visit this evening,' he said to Saddler. 'Around eight o'clock. All right?'

There was still plenty of daylight when they arrived in the street where Kirby lived, though a fine drizzle was falling.

'It's the fourth house along on the left,' Saddler observed, as he switched off the windscreen wipers, followed by the ignition.

They walked the short distance and paused at the top of the basement steps. A light shone somewhere inside, though the front room was in semi-darkness. With a nimbleness defying his size, Saddler descended the steps.

'Watch out, sir, they're slippery,' he said to his chief inspector who cautiously followed him.

Cain pressed the bell and they both stood back and waited.

'Who is it?' a disembodied voice asked.

Startled, they glanced toward a small grille let into the wall beside the door from where the voice had come.

'It's Detective Chief Inspector Cain and Detective Sergeant Saddler,' Cain replied.

A moment later the door opened to reveal Kirby in a pair of jeans and an ancient khaki shirt.

'I'm redecorating the bathroom,' he said, 'but come in if you want.'

Cain noticed that the front door was equipped with a number of security devices, which might be no more than normal prudence in the circumstances.

Kirby switched on a light in the front room and went over to the window to draw the curtains.

'Might as well shut out this foul evening,' he remarked. 'It's a bit like being in a goldfish bowl down here. Everyone looks in as they pass and all you see in return are legs of all sizes. Anyway, Chief Inspector, what brings you here unheralded?' His tone was faintly hostile and he perched himself on the arm of a chair as if to emphasise they were unwelcome guests.

'How well did you know Joe Gillfroy?' Cain asked, having decided on a blunt approach. Kirby was not somebody with whom to beat about the bush, being well versed in the interrogation game, which he had learned in a tough police force.

'Oh, so that's why you're here,' Kirby said with a touch of scorn. 'I scarcely knew him at all.'

'But well enough to give him your telephone number,' Cain broke in.

'If you'll just listen, I'll explain. Gillfroy was an associate of Ruding, a pretty worthless individual, though presumably he had his uses as far as Ruding was concerned. I don't pretend to understand what binds criminals together. Anyway, Ruding brought Gillfroy here one evening. I was furious and showed it in no uncertain terms.' He glared at Cain. 'And that's the only time I ever met Gillfroy.'

'Did you give him your telephone number?'

'I certainly did not. Ruding must have done so.'

'I wonder why?' Cain said in a speculative tone.

'I can't help you.'

'Did Gillfroy ever call you?'

'No. He'd have got exceedingly short shrift if he had.'

'Do you now regret having used Ruding to burgle Bilak's flat?'

'Of course. It's nearly cost me my job and may yet do that. The whole venture was a disaster.' He gave Cain a baleful look. 'But I imagine the police also have plans that sometimes go awry. Unfortunately, in both our jobs one is obliged on occasions to rely on basically unreliable people. Ruding's credentials as a cat burglar were of the highest, but that didn't prevent him mischief-making when it suited his purpose.'

'Are you referring to his attempt to get you to give evidence at his trial?'

'Yes.'

111

'I can't say I blame him for that.'

'I told him he could trust me, but that he had to remain silent. But he wouldn't listen. In the event, he managed to stir up a giant hornet's nest and has ended up dead.'

Cain stared at the MI5 man. 'Are you saying that his death was a direct result of what had gone before?'

'No, that wasn't what I meant. I've no idea who killed him or why.' Kirby's tone was sharp and defensive.

'Presumably you have a theory or two about who killed him,' Cain said.

'It's fairly obvious to me that it was a gang killing. Ruding fell out with one of the barons and was murdered.'

'Motive?'

'Your guess is probably better than mine. I understand there's a man named Grigg whom Ruding associated with and who played in the big crime league.'

'Ever meet him?'

'Good heavens, no. I only know his name through Ruding.'

'How many meetings did you have with Eddie Ruding to set up the Bilak burglary?'

Kirby gave the Yard officer a suspicious look. 'I don't really remember.'

'Would you have a record? Entries in your diary, that sort of thing?'

Kirby shook his head. 'I never make any written record of that sort of operation.'

'So, roughly, how many times did you meet him before the burglary?'

'Four in all, I think.'

'All of them here at your flat?'

'Look, Chief Inspector, I answered all these questions the first time you interviewed me.'

Cain nodded. 'I'm sure it's also your experience that interrogations can become repetitious,' he said with an edge to his voice. 'So where did these meetings with Ruding take place?'

112

'Two were in a pub in Vauxhall Bridge Road and two here.'

'What was the name of the pub?'

'The King's Hussar.'

'And it was on one of the visits here he brought Gillfroy?'

'Yes.'

'Did he say why he'd brought a friend?'

'He didn't have to. It was a ploy to get me to use him.'

'Presumably he told you what expertise Gillfroy had to offer?'

'He just said that he was good at surveillance work as nobody ever gave him a second glance.'

'That all?'

'Yes.'

'Extraordinary.'

'It was more than that. It was diabolical and I very nearly gave Ruding his marching orders on the spot.' He paused. 'Any more questions?'

'Not for the moment,' Cain said, standing up. 'We'll leave you to get on with your redecoration.'

'I don't like that fellow,' Saddler said when they were back in their car. 'He lacks humanity.'

Cain gave him a surprised glance. 'Is that shrewd perception or merely a bit of prejudice?'

'It's instinct.'

'Does your instinct go further and tell you whether he's a murderer?'

'I'm afraid not.'

'Pity.'

Chapter 17

Rosa decided to wait a day or two before calling Chief Inspector Cain. Anyway, there was nothing to prevent him phoning her.

In the event, it was the morning after his visit to Colin

Kirby that she asked Stephanie to try and get him on the line. She was always mildly surprised to find police officers actually at their desks, but on this occasion she was in luck.

'I thought I ought to let you know,' she said, 'that I've been to Joe Gillfroy's address in Conna Street and taken possession of his belongings. That is, those you hadn't removed.'

'On whose authority did you do that?' Cain enquired.

'Joe's. He sent me the keys to the house and a letter asking me to look after things for him. It was held up in the post and arrived after his death. I went to Conna Street the same day and was told by the landlord that the police had already been there and had taken away some of his stuff . . .'

'I'd like to see the letter he sent you,' Cain broke in.

'It's in my office if you care to send someone to collect it. I'll keep a photocopy for my file. Was there anything of interest in what you took away?'

'There was a small red notebook with a lot of writing in it. Phone numbers and that sort of thing. We've checked on them, but there are none of any significance.' He didn't propose telling her that Kirby's number was amongst them. 'In truth, we're not much further forward than we were at the beginning. We've had no good leads. I doubt whether we'll get far until we've discovered a motive.'

'What about Grigg? Didn't he have a motive?'

'You tell me, Miss Epton. Anyway, Grigg has disappeared.'

'Surely that's significant?'

'Maybe, maybe not.' After a pause he said, 'Will you be responsible for arranging Gillfroy's funeral?'

'I suppose so. Did you find any money amongst his possessions?'

'There was a Post Office Savings Account book showing a credit of seventeen pounds and fifty-six pence.' After a further pause, he said, 'There is something you can do for me, Miss Epton. Arrange a meeting with Mrs Ruding. Will you do that?'

'Why can't you just go and see her?'

'Because she doesn't wish to talk to the police and I don't want to be heavy-handed about it. We could meet in your office, if you're agreeable, and, as far as I'm concerned, you're welcome to sit in on the interview.'

'All right, I'll do what I can.'

'I'd be grateful. Meanwhile, I'll send someone round to collect Gillfroy's letter.'

'He can also collect a piece of paper I found in one of Joe's pockets.'

'What's it say?'

'It has various dates written on it with sums of money opposite them. See what you make of it.'

'And what do *you* make of it?'

'I'll tell you when we meet. Don't raise your hopes, but it could be a small piece of the jigsaw.'

She rang off before Cain could ask why, in that event, she had not let him have it immediately. The answer was that she had only just begun to see its possible significance.

To Rosa's surprise Mrs Ruding raised no serious objection to meeting Cain in Snaith and Epton's office. She had expected to have to deploy all her powers of persuasion.

'I'll come as long as you're there,' Mrs Ruding had said after Rosa explained.

'I will be.'

'All right. Tomorrow afternoon will suit me.'

Fortunately it also suited Cain, who said he would come along at four thirty.

Mrs Ruding arrived first and was ushered into Rosa's room by Ben. She was dressed entirely in black, which Rosa could only assume was done to set the correct tone for the meeting. Clamped on her head was a small black toque beneath which her hair stuck out all round, like flames from a damped-down fire.

She seated herself on the edge of Rosa's visitors' chair and glanced about her without any sign of pleasure.

'I expect Mr Cain will be here in a minute,' Rosa remarked. 'How did you come?'

'By bus.'

Having answered the question, Mrs Ruding showed no inclination to make further conversation. Fortunately, Stephanie announced the arrival of Chief Inspector Cain and Sergeant Saddler.

Cain advanced on Mrs Ruding and held out his hand. After slight hesitation, she gave it a brief shake, letting go as if it was contaminated. Rosa glanced at her trio of visitors, feeling like a hostess faced with unpredictable guests.

'Whatever view you may have of the police, Mrs Ruding,' Cain said, 'I do assure you that I and the officers working with me are committed to bringing to justice the person who murdered your son. I believe you could help us in our task.'

'What do you want to know?' she asked with a disdainful sniff.

'When was the last time you saw Eddie?'

'In prison a few days after 'is trial.'

'Did you see him after he was released from prison?'

'No.'

'But he talked to you on the phone?'

'Yes.'

'And it was he who asked you to leave home and move to a flat in Hounslow?' She nodded and Cain went on, 'He must have given you some idea why he wanted you to move?'

'So I wouldn't be bothered by the newspapers.'

'Is that what he said?'

'I got messages from 'im and from 'is friends. Eddie 'isself spoke to me a couple of times.'

'Did he not tell you where he was staying?'

'Just that 'e was with friends and 'e'd see me soon.'

'Who were these friends?'

'They was Eddie's friends. I don't ask who.'

'Did he not tell you what he was doing?'

'No and I never asked 'im. I just told 'im to be careful.'

'Were you surprised when you discovered he was out of prison?'

'No, because I knew 'e was innocent.'

'Did he have any enemies?'

'Everybody liked my Eddie.'

'Did he tell you he was going to Amsterdam?'

'No. 'E knew it would upset me.'

'I don't follow you, Mrs Ruding.'

''E knew I didn't like 'im seeing 'is brother who lived there. Vincent's a bad lot even if 'e is my son. 'E took after 'is father.'

Cain nodded, as if he fully understood the situation. Rosa for her part knew all about family feuds, but found it hard to regard them with any sympathy.

'Tell me, Mrs Ruding, do you have any evidence that could help us identify your son's murderer?'

'I've already said who done it. That Grigg.' Her tone was like a judgement carved on a tablet of stone.

Cain sighed. 'Police forces all over the world have been alerted to let us know if they have any sightings of Grigg. But even when he's traced, we still need evidence in order to charge and convict him. He's not likely to help us by confessing.'

Mrs Ruding appeared thoughtful for a moment. ''Is cousin, Alex Cartwright, could tell you where 'e is,' she said.

'He says he doesn't know.'

''E's a liar like all that family.'

'What do you know about him?' Cain asked, leaning forward.

''E was one of the ones that phoned me about my Eddie, saying 'e was all right.'

'Are you quite sure about that?' Cain said with rekindled interest.

''E spoke to me first, before my Eddie spoke to me. Said I wasn't to worry as Eddie was being looked after by friends.'

'You recognised Cartwright's voice?'

'Yes.'

'What did you assume from the conversation?'

'That Eddie was in tow with Tam Grigg.'

'He never said that himself when he spoke to you later?'

''E wouldn't would 'e? 'E knew 'ow I felt about Grigg.'

After a pause, Cain said, 'That could prove to be a very important piece of information you've just given us, Mrs Ruding.'

'You'll 'ave to put the thumbscrews on 'im before 'e'll admit it.'

'If necessary, will you stand up in court and swear that Cartwright phoned you about Eddie soon after his release from prison?'

'I'll say anything that 'elps to put Grigg away,' she said.

Shortly afterwards the meeting broke up with Cain thanking Mrs Ruding for her co-operation and Rosa for making the arrangements.

'I hope you're now satisfied that Chief Inspector Cain really means business about finding your son's murderer,' Rosa remarked, as Mrs Ruding prepared to leave.

'Maybe 'e's not as bad as most of 'em,' she said grudgingly. 'But I still want you to keep working for my Eddie's 'onour.' She opened her handbag. ''Ere's some money, take it.'

Rosa shook her head. 'No, you hang on to it. I'll send you an account when we reach the end. It's better that way.'

'Pity it won't be Grigg on the end of a rope.'

She levered herself off her chair and moved toward the door.

'There's one question I'd like to ask you,' Rosa said. 'Why did you never tell me that Grigg's cousin phoned you about Eddie?'

'I thought I 'ad,' she replied without turning round.

118

Rosa watched her retreating back. She's a dangerous and vindictive old woman, she reflected.

Peter Chen lay with his head resting on Rosa's lap. She had cooked him a meal at her flat and had recounted the day's events.

'I wouldn't worry about it too much,' he said, holding her hand against his forehead. 'The police'll go and see this Cartwright fellow and he'll tell them that Mrs Ruding is a lying old cow and that he never spoke to her on the phone and never had any contact with Eddie after his release from prison.'

'I still don't like to feel I've been used.'

'It must happen all the time with the sort of clients you have.'

'Thank you very much.'

'Don't get in a huff. It's an occupational hazard. You're very good at your job, that's all you need to remember. It may be true that Cartwright did phone the old girl.'

'She quite definitely never told me he had.'

He pulled her head down and gave her a kiss. She felt her heart skip a beat. There was something very potent about Peter's kisses.

For the next few minutes, neither of them spoke. Later Rosa said, 'I can't help having doubts about Mrs Ruding's motives. There she is, always telling me how her Eddie trusted me and told her to come and see me if anything happened to him and yet it's the same Eddie who contrived to have me pushed under a tram. It doesn't make sense, Peter.'

'It makes sense if you accept that Eddie himself wasn't a party to the tram incident. He may even have tried to dissuade his accomplices from attempting it, but was ignored.'

'You mean, when he told them who I was, it was they who decided I was a threat?'

'Yes.'

'But I didn't even know them.'

'You were linked to Eddie and they decided to pre-empt any action you might take as a result of seeing them.'

'I wonder if Vincent Ruding was involved in some way.'

'Quite possibly.'

Rosa let out a sigh. 'You're not in a hurry to go home, are you,' she said in a dreamy tone.

'As long as I'm in my office by eight thirty tomorrow morning,' he said, giving her a lingering look.

A few minutes before eight o'clock the next morning, Cain and Saddler arrived outside the Cartwrights' bungalow on the outskirts of Croydon. It was one of six recent constructions in an enclave off a main road.

'Looks as if we've missed him,' Cain remarked crossly, as he saw the empty garage with its doors wide open. 'If we'd come any earlier, we'd have been accused of behaving like secret police knocking on people's doors at dawn. Now he's probably out for the day.'

They walked up the short paved path to the front door and rang the bell. Nothing happened and they were about to return to the car when the door opened and a blonde woman stood there in her dressing-gown. She looked them up and down with an expression of annoyance.

'Mrs Cartwright?' Cain said.

'Yes. No need to ask who you are. You're police.'

Cain made introductions and went on, 'Is your husband at home, Mrs Cartwright?'

'He left about fifteen minutes ago. He's gone round to my sister's place. We're keeping an eye on it while she and her husband are away. Alex goes round every morning.'

'Then we'll catch him there, if you'll give us the address.'

'He's not in any trouble, is he?' she asked with a frown.

'We just want to clear up a few details in connection with Eddie Ruding's death. Your husband knew him.'

'Who my husband knows and doesn't know is his concern. I don't interfere.'

'Would you happen to know where Tam Grigg is?'

'I don't like Tam and he doesn't like me, but I still wouldn't tell you, even if I knew the answer. Give us a piece of paper and I'll write down my sister's address. It's only a couple of miles from here.'

'A tough cookie,' Saddler observed as they drove away.

'And one who knows which side her bread is buttered on,' Cain replied. 'We can probably expect Cartwright to be standing outside the door waiting for us.'

As they walked up the path of the house whose address Mrs Cartwright had given them, they could see Alex on the telephone in the front room.

'That'll be his wife talking to him now,' Cain remarked.

'It's the helluva conversation for a couple who only parted company a short time ago,' Saddler observed as they watched through the window.

Alex Cartwright had his back to them and seemed totally absorbed in his telephone call.

'I don't believe he's talking to his wife,' Cain said with sudden interest. 'Let's knock on the window and see what happens.'

Stepping over a flowerbed, he rapped sharply on the glass. Cartwright looked round with an expression of irritation which changed dramatically when he saw who his visitors were. His jaw fell open and he turned quickly away, at the same time replacing the telephone receiver with startling abruptness. Cain and Saddler exchanged meaningful glances.

'Sorry to interrupt your phone call,' Cain said when, a few seconds later, Cartwright opened the front door. 'Wouldn't have bothered, except you seemed to be going on a bit. Care to tell us who you were talking to?'

'It was a personal matter.'

'Not Tam Grigg by any chance? Telling him whether to come home or stay away a bit longer.'

Cartwright licked his lips, then appeared to decide that bluster was his best option.

121

'You've no right to come bursting in like this. It's an invasion of privacy.'

'So you were speaking to Tam! Pity you rang off so abruptly or you could have given him the latest news. Anyway, where is Tam?'

'I don't know.'

'If that was a foreign call, we can probably find out the details from ever-helpful Telecom.' Cain glanced round the room. 'So this is where you come to phone him? Your wife said you came here every morning. She didn't mention that one of the objects of your visit was to make phone calls, but perhaps she didn't know. We want to have a word with you, Alex, and this seems as good a place as any. Nice and quiet and I take it we're not likely to be disturbed.'

A reluctant Alex Cartwright led the way into the room in which they had watched him on the phone. As they entered, Saddler let out a soft exclamation and stretched out his hand for a piece of paper on the table beside the telephone.

'This the number you were calling, Alex?' he enquired, handing it to Cain.

'010 is the international code,' Cain remarked, 'and I'm almost sure that 33 is the code for France. Are you going to tell us whereabouts in France Tam is staying?'

'Get stuffed!'

'Not until we've put you through the mincing machine,' Cain replied equably. 'We'll come back to this number later, but first I want to ask you a few questions about Eddie Ruding. I believe you phoned his mother soon after Eddie came out of prison. Is that right?'

'I don't know what you're talking about.'

'You are acquainted with the lady, aren't you?'

'You've no right to be here. I refuse to answer any questions.'

'We have every right. Your wife gave us the address and you invited us in. Incidentally, if you hadn't talked to Tam for so long, I'm sure she would have warned you we were on our way.'

122

Cartwright scowled, but said nothing.

'Of course,' Cain went on, 'if you prefer, we can transfer this interview to the local nick. It's up to you. Which is it to be?'

Alex Cartwright gave a martyred shrug, which Cain took to be an acknowledgement of defeat, at least for the time being. He repeated his question.

'I may have phoned her,' Cartwright said sullenly. 'It's not yet a crime to speak to someone on the phone, is it?'

'Mrs Ruding says you called her to say that Eddie was all right and being looked after by friends. Is that correct?'

'So what?'

'Was it Tam who was taking care of Eddie at the time?'

'May have been.'

'Where?'

Cartwright gave a helpless shrug. 'At his home.'

'Tam's home?'

'There's a flat over his garage. He was doing Eddie a kindness. Eddie got in touch with him when he came out.'

'How long did he stay in Tam's flat?'

'Two or three days, then he just upped and left without a word. He was there one minute and gone the next.'

'Presumably that was when he took off for Amsterdam?'

'I don't know anything about that.'

'Did he get in touch with Tam again when he returned from Holland?'

'No.'

'How do you know?'

'Because I do know. The next I heard of Eddie was when I read about his death.'

'Did Tam murder him?'

'Tam was his friend. He wouldn't do a daft thing like that.'

'Was he also Joe Gillfroy's friend?'

'Tam didn't kill him either.'

'So why's he skipped the country?'

'He didn't want to be harassed by you lot.'

'Look, Alex, there are a lot of people who believe

123

Tam committed both murders. Karate chops to the neck are the sort of thing he practises in that gym of his. The point is that you'd be doing yourself a favour by telling us all you know. I can't make any promises about your future prospects, except to say they'd certainly be improved by co-operating with us now. I can't see Tam behaving with much chivalry if it became a question of you or him.'

'I've told you all I know. Tam went away because he believed he was being set up.'

'Who by?'

'Eddie's mother. She's always hated Tam and she's as ruthless as anything you'll find in a jungle. This has been her chance to get back at him.'

Cain didn't doubt that Mrs Ruding was capable of the sort of mischief that verged on criminality. But equally he didn't see Grigg as the hapless victim of an old lady's spite. Wherever the truth lay, it was imperative that he should interview Tam Grigg himself.

'Mind if I use the phone?' he asked. Cartwright shrugged, but his nonchalance quickly gave way to alarm as he watched Cain unfold the piece of paper that bore Grigg's number. He made a small strangulated sound as Cain began to dial.

'Looks as if he's gone out,' Cain said half a minute later, to Cartwright's obvious relief. 'You'll have quite a lot to tell him when you next speak together, won't you? Advise him to come home.' Cain paused. 'Within the next twenty-four hours unless he wants us to get the French police to smoke him out.'

Chapter 18

Even the parrot fell silent in mid-squawk when Vincent Ruding's visitor arrived.

'I've come for the money,' the man said in his accented English.

'I keep on telling you, I don't have it. The police took it off my brother when he was arrested.'

'And I'm tired of hearing you say that. But it's your responsibility now that your brother is dead.'

'I haven't got the money and it's certainly not my responsibility. Why don't you get in touch with the police?'

'We don't deal with your police,' the man said in a harsh voice. 'We've been very patient, but now we are getting tired of your excuses.' He gave Vincent an unfriendly smile. 'We will allow you six more days and that is final. Either you hand over the six thousand pounds your brother took or . . .' He made a throat-cutting gesture.

Ruding swallowed hard. He wished he had never become involved in any of Eddie's shenanigans. Moreover, he was frightened. He knew that the man staring at him with crocodile eyes didn't indulge in idle threats.

'Surely we can come to some arrangement,' he said in a placatory tone.

'Yes, you pay the money.'

'But I don't have it.'

'You have six days to get it.'

'That's impossible.'

The man shrugged. 'Milos needs it or maybe he loses everything. Our boss is not pleased with him and it is all your brother's fault.'

'Supposing I go to the police.'

'Which police?'

'Here in Amsterdam.'

'And what would you tell them?'

'That I'm being threatened by an agent of a foreign intelligence service.'

'Which service from which country?' the man asked in a jeering tone. 'You know nothing about me.'

'You're a colleague of Bilak's.'

'So?'

'You tried to kill my brother's lawyer by pushing her under a tram.'

'You can prove that, yes?'

'Eddie told me.'

'Ah! Eddie told you. Then he will send his testimony from beyond the grave, yes?' In a malevolent tone he went on, 'You are more stupid than I thought. Others decided it was in Eddie's interest to arrange a little accident for his lady lawyer.' He shrugged. 'But it failed. The young man on the bicycle lost his nerve at the last minute and didn't push her hard enough.' He paused. 'But if you think that will interest the police, forget it. You, my friend, are in no position to go to the police about anything.' He rose and walked to the door. 'Six days, that's how long you have to find the money.'

'How can I possibly find six thousand pounds in that time?' Ruding asked in an anguished voice.

The man stared at him thoughtfully for a moment. 'Drug peddlers can always find money,' he said with a sneer.

The parrot screeched and ruffled its feathers. Vincent Ruding sat down heavily as if he had been felled.

It was crazy their putting pressure on him to produce the money. The whole thing had become a nightmare since Eddie's death. His brother had told him how on his release from prison he had been approached by someone claiming to be a friend of Bilak who said he had a proposition to put to him. The only snag was that it required a visit to Amsterdam, all expenses paid. Eddie asked why Amsterdam and was told that the man who was actually going to put the proposition was based in Holland and didn't wish to set foot in England. In these circumstances Eddie didn't regard an

126

all-expenses-paid trip as an imposition. More like a bonus, in fact.

All this Eddie had related to his brother when he arrived in the city. He had been staying under Tam Grigg's roof for a few days, but never felt comfortable in his company and was glad to get away.

He told Vincent how Rosa Epton had spotted him in the café on Leidseplein and how upset his companions had been when he mentioned it to them. One had immediately left the table to follow the solicitor and her Chinese boyfriend. Later, when he heard about the tram incident, it was his turn to be upset. He had come to Vincent's flat that same evening.

Though Eddie himself wasn't in the drugs racket, he had once or twice acted as a courier for his brother. He had, however, always refused to become more heavily involved.

Vincent had been a distributor ever since he got married. His Javanese father-in-law was a member of a cartel with ramifications all over the Orient. Amsterdam was its European centre of operations.

As he sat brooding on the sofa, the parrot watched him with beady-eyed interest. It was hoping for a piece of its favourite apple, but Vincent showed no sign of moving and it was probably as well that the bird was unable to read his thoughts.

It seemed there might be only one way out of his predicament. A wild animal is at its most dangerous when cornered and the same goes for the human species in certain circumstances.

It is important to be able to recognise the circumstances. Eddie and Joe Gillfroy had both failed to do so and had ended up dead.

It was on the previous day that Peter suggested to Rosa they should visit Amsterdam again.

'I think you ought to talk to Vincent Ruding. I'm certain he can tell us more about his brother's death.'

'What makes you think he'll be prepared to talk?' Rosa asked.

'It's worth a try.'

'I can't possibly justify the expense, Peter. I could scarcely charge it up to Mrs Ruding, and Robin would dissolve our partnership if I suggested the firm should absorb the cost. It's not on.'

Peter nodded. 'I thought that might be your reaction, so we'll make a weekend of it and I'll pay. We'll fly over on Saturday and come back Sunday evening.'

'Weekend flights are usually fully booked at this time of year,' she said in a doubtful voice.

'I already have the tickets. Also a reservation at the same hotel as before. Any further objections?'

Rosa looked at him with a mixture of desire and exasperation.

'And supposing he's not there?' she asked in a faintly querulous tone.

'Then we'll have more time to enjoy ourselves.'

'Wouldn't it be better to phone and find out if he'll be at home?'

'Much better to surprise him if we can. If he's not at home on Saturday, there's still Sunday. Anyway, he's a caretaker and they spend more time on their premises than most people.'

'What time is our flight?' Rosa asked as she finally capitulated.

'Midday from Gatwick.'

She had known all along that she would capitulate, though a combination of emotions had compelled her to put up a fight of sorts. The trouble was that Peter knew her too well. And she did love him, even though she continued to reject his proposals of marriage.

Two days later they arrived at Schipol airport and took a taxi into the city.

'I suggest we check in at the hotel and then make our way to Jutenbergerstraat,' Peter said. 'With luck he'll be at home watching sport on TV, same as he'd be doing if he were in England.'

Their taxi crossed a canal and a moment later they found themselves in Leidseplein with the art nouveau American Hotel on their left.

'Not nervous, are you?' he asked, taking her hand in his.

She shook her head. 'I don't think I'll ever again regard trams with any affection.'

'You'd like Hong Kong ones,' he said solemnly. 'They're stately contraptions with a lower and an upper deck. But we'll stick to taxis on this trip.'

Ninety minutes later a taxi put them down outside Vincent Ruding's block of flats. Peter asked the driver to wait while he ascertained whether the person they had come to see was at home.

The street door was closed and Peter pressed the bell of the caretaker's basement flat. The intercom crackled into life and a wary voice enquired in Dutch who was there.

'It's him,' Peter whispered to Rosa before turning back to the grille from which the voice had emerged. 'It's Rosa Epton, your brother's solicitor. She'd like to talk to you, Mr Ruding.'

It seemed an age before anything happened, then there was a short buzz and the street door clicked open. Leaving Rosa to prevent it closing again, Peter dashed back to their taxi to pay off the driver.

Vincent Ruding was standing by his half-open door when they reached the bottom of the stairs. He was unshaven and looked generally unkempt.

'We met briefly at Eddie's funeral,' Rosa said with a quick smile.

'I remember.'

'I'd very much like to have a talk with you, if it's convenient. You know Peter Chen, of course.'

He opened the door fully and stood aside to let them in. The parrot gave a couple of squawks as they entered the living-room before deciding they weren't worth further attention.

'What do you want to talk about?' Ruding asked, following them into the room.

'I believe you know more about your brother's death than you've so far told anyone.'

'If you're suggesting I killed him, you're wrong.'

'I'm not suggesting that at all, but I believe you may hold a clue to his death.'

'If you want my opinion, I think he was killed by the people who are now threatening me.'

Rosa stared at him in surprise. 'What people are you talking about?'

In nervous, halting sentences, he told them of the recent visit he had received, which was the culmination of a series of threats.

'If anyone ought to pay over the money my brother took, it should be you,' he said. 'I don't mean personally, but as my brother's solicitor. Why can't you ask the police to hand it over to you?'

'Apart from anything else, it's stolen money. It didn't belong to your brother and doesn't form part of his estate.' She paused. 'But you really believe Eddie was caught up in some spy deal?'

'It figures. He came over to Amsterdam to be propositioned.'

'Would he have consented to work for a foreign intelligence service?'

Vincent Ruding smiled sourly. 'If the money was good, why not? Especially after the way he'd been treated by MI5.'

'MI5 got him out of prison.'

'They also got him in. Kirby was ready to use Eddie and then throw him to the wolves.'

'Is that how Eddie felt?'

'It's how I'd have felt in his place.'

'I get the impression that you and Eddie got on quite well?'

130

'We were OK together.'

'Despite your mother?'

'She doted on Eddie as much as she hated me.'

'Why did she hate you?'

'Because I liked my father and took his side when they broke up, she wrote me off.' He gave a half-smile in reflection. 'She'd have killed Eddie if she'd found out how much we kept in touch. She's a very jealous woman is our Charlotte.'

'Do you believe Tam Grigg had anything to do with Eddie's death?'

Ruding stared into the middle distance for a few moments. 'I warned Eddie more than once to stay clear of Grigg. He wasn't in Tam's league, even if he liked to think he was.' He turned his gaze back to Rosa. 'That doesn't answer your question, but it's all I'm saying.'

The telephone rang and he glared at it as if hoping it would stop. When it didn't, he walked across the room and lifted the receiver. He said something in Dutch, then switched to English.

'OK. Eight o'clock. Usual place,' he said curtly and rang off.

When he turned round he frowned, as if Rosa and Peter had crept in while his back was turned.

'I have to go out,' he said abruptly and walked toward the door.

'Bye, bye,' the parrot screeched as everyone prepared to depart.

Peter, who had the priceless gift of securing taxis in foreign cities, had soon found one and given the driver the name of their hotel.

'Not a wholly wasted journey,' he remarked as the cab pulled away from the kerb. 'At least he threw fresh light on Eddie's activities.'

'And inadvertently on his own,' Rosa replied.

'I'm not with you.'

'There was a magazine sticking out beneath the parrot's

131

cage. I pulled it out a bit further when he was on the phone. The cover depicted kinky sex.'

'You can't draw any conclusions from that. Not in Amsterdam.'

'It tells one something about his tastes. And don't forget that the person who murdered Eddie and Joe was a pervert.'

'There's no evidence he was a sexual pervert.'

'A pervert is a pervert,' Rosa said firmly.

That evening they had dinner at an Indonesian restaurant not far from the flower market. Rosa was feeling relaxed and left Peter to do the ordering. As she found the menu incomprehensible, she didn't have much choice.

'We'll start with *satay*,' he said, after considerable deliberation. 'Then I suggest *sambal ikan goreng* with a side order of *gado gado* and finally the ice *kachang* is a must.' He met Rosa's bemused expression. 'The starter is bits of chicken on a bamboo skewer which comes with a spicy peanut sauce. I think you'll like it.'

'Go on.'

'The main course is fish fried in a chilli paste and *gado gado* is an Indonesian salad with prawn crackers and peanut dressing.'

'And the ice *kachang* which is a must?'

'It's a mound of crushed ice smothered in coconut milk and tropical fruit juices. It's delicious.'

'Even without peanuts?'

Peter gave her a reproachful look. 'You'd live on sausage and mash and bread-and-butter pudding, if it weren't for me,' he said.

'And be the size of a hot-air balloon,' she remarked with a laugh.

During the meal they talked about everything save the matter that had brought them to Amsterdam, but with the arrival of coffee they fell to discussing their visit to Vincent Ruding that afternoon.

'I think you're barking up the wrong tree if you regard Ruding's possession of a kinky magazine as evidence of the

132

sort of perversion that could make him a murderer,' Peter said as he sipped a cup of very strong coffee. 'Whatever motive anyone had for killing Eddie and Joe, it certainly wasn't a sexual one. Kinky magazines may inflame their kinky readers, but there was no hint of kinkiness in either of the murders. They had their necks broken by a karate chop.'

'You don't call it kinky that Eddie's body was deposited outside a prison and Joe's left on top of Eddie's grave?'

'Bizarre, but not kinky.'

'But you agree it was the work of a pervert?'

'The murderer would appear to have a twisted mind.'

'A pervert, in fact.'

'But not a sexual pervert. There's absolutely no evidence that either murder was committed from a sexual motive.'

'Would you eliminate Ruding from your list of suspects?'

'Without proof of motive, he wouldn't have been on it in the first place.'

Rosa was thoughtful for a while. 'Do you think it's possible the two brothers were involved in something together?'

'Anything's possible,' Peter said with a sigh. He pushed back his chair. 'Let's stroll back to the hotel.'

Rosa seemed heavily preoccupied as they walked arm in arm on a warm, balmy night.

'A penny for your thoughts,' Peter said eventually.

'I'm trying to decide whether Joe misled me,' Rosa replied. 'Deliberately misled me.'

Chapter 19

On Monday morning Rosa went straight to court and didn't arrive in the office until mid-afternoon. She had told Robin that she was going away with Peter for the weekend, but hadn't mentioned Amsterdam as this would have involved her in more explanation than she was prepared to offer.

'Mr Kirby's been on the phone,' Stephanie said as Rosa entered the outer office. 'I told him you'd be back sometime this afternoon.'

'Does he want me to call him?' Rosa asked, more than a little surprised by the news.

'No. He refused to leave his number and said he'd phone back later.'

Rosa had been at her desk for about half an hour when Stephanie announced that Colin Kirby was on the line.

'Miss Epton? I wonder if we could meet in the near future? I have a favour to ask of you.'

'Can't you tell me over the phone?'

'It would be better if we met. It won't take long. Is this evening possible?'

Rosa was torn between curiosity and not wishing to appear too obliging. After all, she owed Kirby nothing. Even if he had instigated Eddie's release from prison, he had earlier been downright unhelpful.

'Where do you suggest we meet?' she asked, when curiosity had gained the upper hand.

'Do you know Pierre's Bar at the rear of Harrods?'

'No, but I can probably find it.'

'Could we meet there at six thirty?'

'All right.'

'And Miss Epton? I'd be grateful if you didn't tell anyone.'

'I wouldn't have thought you were in a position to lay down terms,' Rosa said.

'Point taken. I'll see you at six thirty at Pierre's.'

It was five minutes after the half-hour when Rosa arrived. She spotted Kirby sitting alone at an alcove table, staring morosely into a glass of beer. Though she had never met him before, he was immediately recognisable from the description Eddie had given her. His short grizzled hair gave him a generally severe expression. He was not somebody one would choose to cross.

He looked up and saw Rosa observing him and gave her

a small flicker of a smile as he half rose. She walked over to join him.

After a quick, almost embarrassed handshake, he said, 'What can I get you? I'm drinking beer, but I don't suppose that appeals to you.'

'I'd like a glass of white wine,' Rosa replied and reached for a peanut from the bowl on their table.

He returned with the wine and sat down opposite her.

'I want your help,' he said, without any preliminary. 'Your help to clear my name with my employer and generally to restore my reputation.'

Rosa stared at him in astonishment. It was the last thing she had expected, even though she had had no clear idea what he might want of her.

'Perhaps I'd better explain,' he went on. 'Ever since the Ruding affair, I've lived under a cloud. I've been interviewed by the police and made to feel like a suspect. Though I'm trained to cope with stress and I'm resilient by nature, life has been unbearable at times. I'm sure you can understand that.'

'Even if I can, I don't see how I can help you,' Rosa said.

'I'd like you to write a letter to the head of my service – even swear an affidavit if you think that would carry more weight – saying that Eddie Ruding never uttered a word in your presence which suggested he was in fear of me as a result of the botched burglary at Bilak's flat.'

Rosa stared in amazement at the austere figure sitting opposite her. How could he possibly think that such a letter could help to restore his reputation?

'Will you do that for me?' he asked.

She took a sip of wine while she tried to assemble her thoughts.

'A letter from me saying that would carry no more weight than one from . . . from the doorman outside.'

'But it is true, isn't it, that he never said anything to suggest he was frightened of me or of what I might do to him?'

135

'He was very upset that you wouldn't give evidence at his trial,' Rosa said in a temporising voice.

'On the other hand, I pulled every possible string to get him out of prison. And look what that has cost me. You've never believed I killed him, have you?' he enquired suddenly.

'I don't know who killed him. Presumably the same person who later murdered Joe Gillfroy.'

Kirby grimaced as if he had been reminded of something distasteful.

'I can see I've not persuaded you that your help would be of value to me.'

'I'm afraid you haven't.' After a pause she went on, 'To be blunt, you had the opportunity to kill Eddie, as indeed, did a lot of other people . . .'

'But what conceivable motive did I have?' he broke in vehemently. 'Of course I had the opportunity. Come to that, I expect you did too! But motive! Whoever murdered Ruding must have had a powerful motive. I didn't have one at all.' He stared angrily into his beer glass. 'As a matter of fact, Ruding had more of a motive to murder me. Before I explain, let me ask you this: do you know how Ruding and I originally met?'

'No.'

'Did you ever ask him?'

'Yes, but he was evasive and I didn't press him.'

Kirby gave her a wintry smile. 'I can understand his not being forthcoming. The official story is that I went to interview a prisoner we were interested in and, while there, met his cell-mate who was Ruding and who was introduced to me as the best cat burglar in London. And that I subsequently approached Ruding on his release to do a job on behalf of the Security Service. That, as I say, is the official story. The truth, however, is more colourful. Before I moved to my present flat, I lived in Fulham. One evening I arrived home to find there'd been a break-in. Moreover, the burglar was still on the premises. No guesses as to who it was.

After I'd tied him up, I had a look around and was impressed by the neat, tidy job he had done. So I struck a bargain with him: either I turned him over to the police or he agreed to work for me when I required his services. It didn't take him long to choose. I made him sign a statement admitting the burglary and I warned him I would use it against him if he ever tried to go back on our deal.' He paused and met Rosa's gaze. 'So you can see he had more reason to murder me than the other way round. I was in effect blackmailing him and blackmailers are the accepted victims of murder.' He paused again. 'Now you know the truth. I've never even told my own superiors what I've just told you. Everyone's aware that the Security Service indulges in dirty tricks from time to time. It's often the only way to get results. Having Ruding on permanent stand-by had its uses. His death has brought me nothing save aggravation.'

Rosa listened intently to what Kirby told her. She was inclined to believe what he had said, for there didn't seem any reason for him to have invented it. What still puzzled her, however, was why he had told her. She was so uncertain what to make of this strange meeting that she remained silent.

Eventually he said, 'I do assure you, Miss Epton, that a letter on the lines I've indicated would help to re-establish my position. I like my job and I've worked hard since I came to the UK. I have to face the fact that the burglary at Bilak's flat was a failure and I'm left to carry the can. If it had been successful, my people would have been delighted and would have brushed off any awkward questions. But when an operation fails, you stand alone.' He gave her a rueful look. 'Has Chief Inspector Cain asked you questions about me?' he said abruptly.

'No. I'd hardly have expected him to.'

'It wouldn't have surprised me if he had. I'm sure he regards it as too much of a coincidence that Ruding was killed so soon after I'd fought to get him out of prison.'

137

'That doesn't make sense. In any event, I have a feeling that Eddie plunged straight back into trouble.'

'Perhaps you'll tell Cain that next time you speak to him.'

Either this is one huge charade, Rosa reflected, or he genuinely thinks I have more clout at my disposal than is the case. She decided it was time to steer the conversation in a fresh direction.

'If neither you nor I killed Eddie, who do you think did?'

'Have you heard of somebody called Tam Grigg?'

'I have indeed.'

'I've been making my own enquiries and I think Grigg is the person whom the police should be questioning. I gather he's missing at the moment, which in itself is suspicious.'

'Joe Gillfroy certainly believed Grigg was a murderer,' Rosa remarked. 'It could be that he said so once too often.'

The bar was filling up, but Kirby managed to attract the attention of a young waiter who was flitting around the tables. He came over to where they were sitting.

'A white wine and a lager,' Kirby said. 'And another bowl of peanuts.' The waiter was about to move away when Kirby produced a £5 note. 'Take this and keep the change.'

'That's very kind of you, sir,' the waiter said. 'I'll fetch your drinks right away.'

Kirby watched him thread his way to the bar. Then turning to Rosa, he said, 'I never mind tipping well when the service deserves it. He's a new face here.'

The waiter returned with their drinks and a fresh bowl of peanuts. 'Here we are and thank you again, sir.'

Rosa hadn't really wanted another drink and had been on the verge of going home. She gazed at her glass with resignation, then annoyance when she reflected that she had not been asked if she wanted it.

Kirby, who had been gazing about the room, now turned his attention back to her.

'You were mentioning Gillfroy,' he said. 'What do you make of his body being left on top of Ruding's grave?'

'Macabre, to say the least.'

'Do you think it had any significance?'

'I think the murderer wanted the world to know that both men had been killed by the same hand.'

'That would be my interpretation, too.'

'I also believe the murderer was a pervert.'

'A pervert?' he said with a frown. 'What makes you say that? There was no evidence of sexual interference.'

'I think the locations of the two bodies reveal a nasty, twisted mind. I call it perverted, you may have some other word for it.' She glanced at her watch and made to get up. 'I'm afraid I must go. I still don't see that I can be of any help to you in the way you suggest, but give me time to think it over. I can find my own way out, so I'll just say goodnight.'

Leaving Kirby staring after her with a thoughtful expression, she pushed her way to the door. She hadn't liked him when he was being unhelpful over Eddie's trial and she didn't like him any better now. He was graceless, even faintly sinister. Moreover, she was still thoroughly perplexed as to the real reason for their meeting. She would have found it easier to accept the reason he had given her if he were a more sympathetic person. As it was, the more she thought about it, the more suspicious she became.

But then the whole affair, comprising as it did two inexplicable and bizarre murders, was one whole steaming dunghill of suspicion.

Chapter 20

Most people who knew him considered that Tam Grigg's anger was something from which to take cover. It was the more intimidating for being icy and perfectly controlled. It was as though the temperature had dropped below zero in a matter of seconds.

Alex Cartwright was therefore thankful that several hundred miles separated him from his cousin when he called to inform Tam that the police had discovered his French telephone number.

Grigg immediately packed his belongings and caught one of the pleasure-steamers that plied the lake. He disembarked at Lausanne on the Swiss side and took a train to Geneva which was less than an hour's run. There he booked into a *pension* and went out to make enquiries about flight departures. The next morning he caught a plane to Dublin. On arrival in the Irish capital he went to a modest hotel and sat down to review his situation.

He had travelled on his Arnold Berger passport and felt in no immediate danger of being traced. After a brisk walk to stretch his leg muscles, he returned to his hotel room and put through a call to Alex.

'It's me,' he said tersely, as soon as he heard his cousin's voice.

'Am I glad to hear from you? I didn't know how to get in touch. Where are you speaking from?'

'It doesn't matter. Have there been any further developments?'

'No, not a thing. Haven't heard anything from Cain since he turned up at Gloria's house. Most unfortunate that! Did he try and call you at the villa?'

'I didn't hang around to find out. Is Shirley there?' he asked in a suddenly suspicious tone.

'No, she's out shopping.'

Grigg grunted. He didn't want Alex's wife overhearing everything they said, not that he intended giving any secrets away on the phone.

'Well, I'll get off the line. It's probably being tapped.'

'Probably,' Cartwright said in a chastened tone.

'Wait till you hear from me.'

'How'll you get in touch, Tam?'

'Leave that to me.'

For the next half-hour Grigg sat on his bed and thought.

140

He had done a lot of thinking in the past thirty-six hours, but was still undecided on his next move. Not that he had that many options. In fact, only two presented themselves. He could stay abroad on Arnold Berger's passport with the odds that it would take quite a while for the law to catch up with him. It was a tempting option, for he had enough money to survive comfortably. But the search for him would be bound to intensify and when eventually he was caught there would be awkward questions to answer. Questions that would grow more awkward with each day that passed.

The other option was to return home and confront the police. That would take the wind out of their sails and point to his innocence. He would say that as soon as he learnt they wished to interview him, he packed his bags and came hurrying back. He would hardly have done that if he had a guilty conscience, he would point out.

The first was the better short-term option, but to give himself up had a more beneficial long-term prospect. Moreover, he was not a fugitive by nature and there were fewer and fewer countries in which one could safely seek refuge.

Accordingly, the next morning found him disembarking from the night ferry at Holyhead and taking a train to Manchester. Three hours after his arrival there, he was on his way to London.

Once he had made up his mind to confront the police, there was no reason why he shouldn't have taken the quickest and most direct route to London. Nothing, that is, save for a natural instinct to cover his tracks, even when there was no real need to do so.

He left his luggage at Euston station and looked for a public telephone.

'Is that you, Alex? It's me.'

'Where are you speaking from?' Alex asked anxiously.

'It doesn't matter.' He no longer minded if the line was being tapped or Alex's wife was listening in on an extension. 'Anything fresh happened since I last spoke to you?'

'Nothing. I gather they're keeping a watch for you at airports and the cross-Channel seaports. That's what Clive Fox wrote in today's *Gazette*. He and the police seem to be scratching one another's backs.'

'Let them,' Grigg said, and rang off before Alex could start asking further questions.

He inserted another coin in the box and rang Scotland Yard. When a voice answered, he said, 'Give me Detective Chief Inspector Cain. I have some important information for him regarding the Ruding case.'

That should produce results, he thought grimly as he waited to be connected.

'Detective Sergeant Saddler here. Can I help you?'

'I asked to speak to Chief Inspector Cain.'

'I'm afraid he's not available at the moment. Who is it speaking?'

'Tam Grigg.'

There were a few seconds of eloquent silence which Grigg grimly enjoyed.

'Where are you speaking from, Tam?' Saddler said when he was armed with paper and pen.

'Not far away. I understand Chief Inspector Cain wants to see me.'

'Are you at home?'

'No.'

'Where then?'

'Not far away, like I said. But I'll have left before you can trace the call, so don't bother. Will Cain be available soon?'

'Yes.'

'Good, then I'll pay you a visit.'

He rang off, pleased with the initiative he had taken and the effect he had produced. It was about fifty minutes later that he approached the Yard's main entrance. He could see Sergeant Saddler hovering on the other side of the glass doors and permitted himself a small smile.

'Good evening, Sergeant,' he said, choosing his moment

to come up behind the officer, who had turned away to speak to somebody at the reception counter.

As they went up in the lift, Grigg said, 'As soon as I heard you wanted to interview me, I came home and here I am.'

'Save it for when we get to the Chief Inspector's room,' Saddler said, giving him an impassive glance.

A couple of minutes later, Saddler knocked on a door and stood aside to let Grigg enter.

'Well, well, this is a surprise,' Cain said, coming forward as if to greet an unexpected, but welcome guest. Neither man, however, made any effort to shake the other's hand. 'Just back from Lake Geneva, are you?'

'When I heard you wanted to see me, I returned.'

'Come straight from the airport, have you?'

'Why don't you get on with what it is you have to say?'

'In a hurry, are you?'

'Look, I didn't have to come back, but I did. If you only want to make small talk, I've got better things to do.'

'Such as?'

'Helping old ladies across the road.'

For half a minute the two men stared at each other in dislike, then Cain looked down at the open file on his desk.

'Is it a fact that you gave Eddie Ruding shelter when he was released from prison?'

'You know it is, so why ask?'

'I'd like to hear it from you.'

'Yes, I did.'

'For how long?'

'He could have stayed as long as he wanted, but he chose to go after a few days.'

'When did you next see him?'

'I never saw him again.'

'We know he went to Amsterdam and then came back to London. He would have got in touch with you on his return.'

143

'Well, he didn't.'

'Were you expecting to hear from him?'

'No.'

'Did you try and get in touch with him?'

'No, again.'

'My information is that you met him in a pub in Walworth Road the evening before he was found dead. What do you say to that?'

'Not true.'

'Moreover, that you and Eddie left the pub together. Is that right?'

'No, it's not. I never met him in a pub, so we couldn't have left it together.'

'You agree it would be significant if it were true?'

'I'm not here to play word games. What I do know is that somebody's out to frame me.'

'Who?'

'I suspect Eddie's mother. She's always hated my guts and she's a spiteful old witch.'

'Why should she want to frame you?'

'Because she thinks I led her precious Eddie astray.'

'And did you?'

'How can you lead the Devil astray?'

'Do you deny going to the pub in Walworth Road?'

'What's its name?'

'Have you ever been to any pub there?'

'Yes.'

'And met Eddie Ruding?'

'Could be. Pubs are handy places for meeting people.'

'Surely you'd remember if you'd met him the evening before his death?'

'Yes and I don't, so I didn't.'

After Rosa had passed this particular item of information to Cain, he had made intensive enquiries at all the pubs in the area, but had drawn a complete blank. It was, therefore, a line of questioning doomed to failure unless Grigg made admissions.

'Where did you go when you left the pub?' Cain asked.

Grigg let out a long-suffering sigh. 'Give it a rest, Chief Inspector. You're only on a fishing expedition and I'm not for catching.'

'How well did you know Joe Gillfroy?' Cain said, hoping that a sudden change of topic might catch Grigg off balance.

'Gillfroy was a pain in the arse, but that doesn't mean I killed him,' Grigg said with a frown. 'He was a parasite who lived off other people.'

'Any ideas as to who might have murdered him?'

'None.'

'And dumped his body on Eddie's grave?'

'Can't help you.'

'Do you agree that it looks as if both men were killed by the same person?'

'I've no idea.'

'But it looks that way, don't you think?'

'Somebody may have wanted it to look that way.'

'Gillfroy was sure you murdered Eddie.'

'I've told you what I thought of Joe Gillfroy. One wouldn't convict a spider of catching a fly on his word. I imagine Eddie's old witch of a mother was behind all the slanders about me. She'd go to any lengths to stir up trouble where I'm concerned.'

'Both Eddie and Joe were killed by karate chops to the neck.'

'So?'

'I believe you're a karate expert.'

'I've learnt various forms of self-defence.'

'Self-defence can easily become aggression.'

Grigg shrugged. 'If you're still suggesting I killed either of them, you're wasting your time.' He got up. 'I came here voluntarily and I've answered your questions and now I'm going.'

'No you're not,' Cain said quietly. 'Just because you walked in voluntarily doesn't mean you can walk out the same way. We're not as naïve as we may look.'

'I demand to see my lawyer,' Grigg said in cold fury.

'I wondered when that was coming,' Cain remarked with a satisfied smile.

Chapter 21

As so often, it was Ben who drew Rosa's attention to an item of news.

'Seen this, Miss E?' he said eagerly when she arrived in the office the next morning.

Rosa took the newspaper he was holding out and read where his thumb indicated.

Man Held for Questioning in Double Murder Enquiry, ran the headline. Beneath came a dozen lines of text:

Scotland Yard has confirmed that a man is being held for questioning in connection with two unsolved murders. That of Eddie Ruding whose body with a broken neck was discovered lying against the wall of Wandsworth Prison and of Joe Gillfroy whose body was found on top of Ruding's grave a few days after his burial. Gillfroy had also died from a broken neck. A spokesman refused to confirm that the man being held is Tam Grigg of Hepple Common near Epsom. It is known, however, that the police have been anxious to trace Grigg, who disappeared from his home ten days ago. It is thought that Grigg may have surrendered himself in the knowledge that the police wished to interview him. No charges have yet been preferred.

Rosa had barely finished reading the piece when Stephanie signalled to her.

'Mrs Ruding wants to speak to you. Mrs Charlotte Ruding,' she added, rolling her eyes heavenwards.

146

'I'll take it in my room,' Rosa said and hurried away.

'Is that Miss Epton?'

'Yes, Mrs Ruding.'

'It's Mrs Charlotte Ruding speaking,' she said with the determination of a runaway train. 'Have you seen a paper this morning?'

'About Tam Grigg, you mean?'

'What I want to know is why they say 'e 'asn't yet been charged.'

'Obviously because the police are still questioning him and aren't yet ready to prefer charges. There's nothing unusual about that.'

'When are they going to charge 'im?'

'I've no idea. It depends on the evidence they have.'

'But Grigg did it. 'E killed my Eddie.'

Rosa sighed. 'But the police still need evidence before they can bring a charge.'

'Huh!' Her tone was full of scorn. She went on, 'If they don't charge Grigg, it'll be because 'e's given them a sweetener.'

'I wouldn't think that for a moment,' Rosa said. 'Anyway, let's wait and see what happens before making any judgements. They'll either have to charge him or let him go. They can't hold him indefinitely.'

'I'd like you to phone that Inspector Cain and tell 'im where 'is duty lies. Otherwise I'll write to my MP. I'll also write to that Clive Fox at the *Morning Gazette*. 'E seems interested in what 'appened to my Eddie.'

'Look, Mrs Ruding, there's nothing any of us can do at the moment. We just have to await developments. Once the police have decided on their next move, we can determine ours.'

Rosa couldn't help hoping that Grigg would be charged, if only to keep Mrs Ruding quiet. It would certainly accord with the popular vote. But then the likes of Tam Grigg seldom had friends. Only henchmen who were often the first to dance on their graves.

147

Gathering up her papers for court, Rosa returned along the corridor to reception. 'If Mrs Ruding phones, tell her you've no idea when I'll be back,' she called out to Stephanie.

'I'll say you've gone to the moon,' Stephanie replied.

Alex Cartwright was stunned when he heard that Tam was being held by the police. The fact that the news came via Frank Lidman, who was Grigg's solicitor, seemed to make it worse.

'I suspect the worst,' Lidman said. 'I always do where the police are concerned. And not without cause. Ever since the Police and Criminal Evidence Act became law, they've been circumventing its provisions, particularly in relation to the rights of somebody held in custody.' He cleared his throat noisily. 'Put me in the picture about Tam. I need to know as much as possible before I go to the station. Where's he been and what's he been up to?'

Succinctness was not Cartwright's strong suit, nor patience Lidman's, but eventually Alex reached the end of his recital of events and Lidman rang off.

'They're trying to frame him, Frank,' Alex had said.

It was a cry that many of Lidman's clients often sent up and he had grown accustomed to hearing it with a certain degree of cynicism.

It was a long time since Tam Grigg had spent a night in a police cell and he had not enjoyed the experience. It had, however, given him time to review his situation. He now realised how seriously he had misjudged it. He had been confident that his voluntary arrival at Scotland Yard without a lawyer in tow would take the wind out of everyone's sails. He had reckoned that if the police had sufficient evidence to justify charging him with murder, they would have obtained an arrest warrant. They had not done so and therefore presumably lacked the necessary evidence. Accordingly, he had assumed that, after answering their questions, he would leave as freely as he had arrived. That was where the misjudgement arose. Moreover, a sleepless night had brought him no comfort. Although he had not been charged, he was still being held. What he would dearly have liked to know was how much evidence they did have against him. His demands to see his lawyer had met with bland assurances that this would be arranged, but nothing seemed to happen. He knew the police were adept at stalling when it suited them, but it did nothing to improve his state of mind.

It was broad daylight when he sank into a dreamless sleep from which he was awakened by the arrival of a Falstaffian breakfast. He gave it a single glance and shuddered.

'Here you are, mate,' said the officer who brought it to his cell. 'Enjoy your breakfast. Not bothered about our cholesterol level, are we?' he added, eyeing the rashers of streaky bacon and the two slices of fried bread, on one of which was perched a glistening fried egg.

'I demand to see my lawyer,' Grigg said.

'I'll let Chief Inspector Cain know.'

'He already does.'

'Then you've nothing to worry about. Anyway, it's not my concern. Now, enjoy your breakfast while it's still hot. I'll be back later to see if you'd like more tea.'

It was about thirty minutes later that Cain and Saddler reappeared.

'Sorry we're a bit late,' Cain said. 'We had to confer with the CPS before we came.'

'Crown Prosecution Service,' Saddler explained.

'I'm sure Tam knows what CPS stands for,' Cain observed.

Grigg scowled. 'I demand to see my solicitor.'

'He should be on his way,' Cain said, cheerfully. 'We had a bit of difficulty getting hold of him and he didn't sound too pleased when we eventually ran him to earth. But six o'clock in the morning is on the early side for a solicitor. Anyway, he said he'd be here as soon as he could. He seemed to imply that as you'd chosen to give yourself

149

up voluntarily without consulting him, he'd come along in his own sweet time.'

Grigg refrained from saying anything. For the moment the police held the initiative and there was nothing he could do about it, apart from concealing his scalded feelings.

'You're sure there's nothing else you want to tell us before Mr Lidman arrives?' Cain asked. For reply, Grigg turned his back on them and Cain went on, 'I thought maybe a night's rest would . . .'

'Save your breath,' Grigg muttered angrily.

Cain smiled and gave Sergeant Saddler a quick wink.

'I reckon he's feeling sorry he came home,' he said, as they left the cell.

'We'd have found him sooner or later.'

'But think of all the trouble he's saved us.'

They had just reached the front hall of the station when the swing-doors flew open as if blown in by a sudden tempest and a small bald-headed man appeared.

'Ah!' he exclaimed on catching sight of the officers.

'Good morning, Mr Lidman,' Cain said.

'Where's my client?'

'I'll get someone to take you to him. I expect you'd like to have a word with him alone and after that we'll meet upstairs in one of the CID offices.'

'If I find, as I very much suspect, that you've been exceeding your powers, you won't have heard the last of it,' the solicitor said in a biting tone.

'Don't try and intimidate me, Mr Lidman. It's a waste of time.'

A few minutes later Lidman was admitted to Grigg's cell.

'Thanks for coming,' Grigg remarked with a touch of sarcasm. 'I got your message.'

'What message?'

'Oh, forget it!' he said with an irritable shrug. 'Now you are here, you can get me out of the place.'

'I take it you've not made any admissions?'

'I haven't yet lost all my marbles.'

'Have you said anything that could be twisted into an admission?'

'Not unless white can be twisted into black.'

'The police are quite capable of it.' Eyeing his client with an air of exasperation, he went on, 'What possessed you to walk into Scotland Yard like a lost child?'

'Because I'm innocent.'

Lidman shook his head as if he found this a wholly unsatisfactory answer. At length he said, 'Well, don't answer any further questions unless I give you the nod. Meanwhile, I'll go and find Cain and tell him we're leaving. We'll take it from there.'

The solicitor found Cain at the end of the passage leading to the cell block.

'I was just coming to see if you were ready,' Cain said.

'Ready for what?'

'For your client to be charged with murder.'

'He never murdered Eddie Ruding.'

Cain smiled. 'That's all right, because he's going to be charged with the murder of Joe Gillfroy.'

Chapter 22

'What do you make of it?' Peter asked, when Rosa arrived at his flat for supper and brought with her an evening paper that carried news of Grigg's arrest. 'Why have they only charged him with Joe's murder?'

'Presumably because they have more evidence in respect of the one than the other. It doesn't mean he won't be further charged, though I rather hope they won't do anything precipitate.'

'What are you trying to say?'

'That I'm not convinced Grigg did murder Eddie.'

151

'Are you suggesting that Eddie and Joe were killed by different people?'

'I'm not suggesting anything. I'm merely saying I'm not convinced that Grigg murdered Eddie.'

'Better not let his mother hear you say that.'

'She'd freak out,' Rosa said with a smile.

'What evidence can Cain have in respect of Joe's death that's missing in the case of Eddie?'

'To begin with, there was Joe's abduction the day before his death when he was driven up to Hampstead and frightened out of his wits. Though if I was defending Grigg, I'd argue that the fact Joe wasn't killed then makes it unlikely Grigg killed him twenty-four hours later.'

'How would the police have evidence of what happened on Hampstead Heath?'

'I passed on to Cain what Joe told me when he came to the office first thing the next morning and my guess would be that the police have managed to get some sort of confirmation. Either from Cartwright or from Grigg's driver-cum-bodyguard. When Grigg showed up at Scotland Yard, all Cain would need would be a provable lie.'

'But you've already advanced an argument against the likelihood of Grigg having murdered Joe.'

Rosa nodded slowly. 'I imagine that Cain has been under immense pressure to produce results. Charging someone with Joe's murder is a sort of halfway house. They'll obviously now do all they can to justify a charge in respect of Eddie Ruding's death. Joe's death is, in a sense, a mere B movie compared with the Eddie extravaganza.'

'Do you still believe both murders were committed by the same person?'

'Definitely.'

'So if you're doubtful whether Grigg killed Eddie, you must also be doubtful about his involvement in Joe's death?'

'Yes.'

'So what are you going to do about it?'

'Nothing for the moment.'

'The paper says that Grigg will appear in court tomorrow. Are you proposing to attend?'

'I've already rearranged my morning in order to do so.'

'I reckon we've talked enough,' Peter said abruptly, drawing her into his side and giving her a long kiss. 'That's just for starters,' he added, as he began to kiss her again.

To Rosa, his kisses could be as intoxicating as champagne cocktails at breakfast-time.

There was a fair-sized crowd milling around in front of the magistrates' court when Rosa arrived. The sight of a television crew had attracted additional bystanders who would not otherwise have paused. Now there was an off chance of their catching a glimpse of themselves on the early evening news. Rosa pushed her way through the crowd toward the main entrance.

'Rosa Epton, isn't it?' a voice said close to her left ear.

She turned her head and saw a youngish man with horn-rimmed spectacles and a determined expression. His voice was vaguely familiar, but his face was totally unknown to her.

'Clive Fox of the *Morning Gazette*,' he went on. 'We spoke on the phone just after Eddie Ruding's murder.'

'I remember.'

'I still find it a fascinating case. Personally, I doubt whether the police have done more than scratch the surface.' He paused. 'Incidentally, in what capacity are you here today?'

'I hold a watching brief,' Rosa replied, and hoped he wouldn't question her further.

'I gather the police are still stuck for evidence in respect of Eddie's death,' Fox went on.

'Presumably, or there'd have been a charge.'

'What's your theory?'

'About what?'

'Ruding's death.'

'If Grigg killed Joe Gillfroy, there's a reasonable inference he also murdered Eddie.'

'Yes, I know all that,' he said with a touch of impatience, 'but what's your personal view? Come on, Miss Epton, let's hear what you really think.'

'Whatever thoughts I have are not for publication.'

He pulled a face. 'Oh, well, have it your own way. My editor has agreed to my doing a full feature on the case once it's over. I might even write a book. I reckon it could be a bestseller. It'll have all the right ingredients. Well, all except one. There's no glamorous girl.'

Rosa laughed. 'I'm sure you'll find one in the wings if you look hard enough.'

'Do you mean that?' he asked eagerly. 'If so, tell.'

Rosa shook her head. 'As far as I'm aware, it's a case without any sexual interest at all.'

'There's no such thing.'

'If we don't get into court soon, we never will,' Rosa said, moving away from his side. She decided that being exposed to Clive Fox's questions was seductive, but risk-laden.

As she pushed her way inside, she wondered if she would see Mrs Ruding in the front row of the public gallery awaiting Grigg's entry with all the zealous expectation of a *tricoteuse*. But a quick look revealed no sign of Eddie's mother. Rosa supposed it was possible that her satisfaction was diminished by the fact he had not been charged with her son's murder. She might at this moment be trying to call Rosa to express her indignation.

Rosa took a seat at one end of the lawyers' bench and gazed around her. It was rather like being at a church wedding, with everyone having a good stare at everyone else.

Frank Lidman, whom she knew slightly, came bursting into court like a small steamroller, with an elderly clerk in attendance carrying his briefcase. Rosa knew from past experience that it contained a number of large tomes which were carried from court to court to intimidate his opponents, who would wonder if there were points of law they had

154

overlooked. The tomes sprouted markers to emphasise the impression.

A thin, harassed-looking man appeared suddenly at Rosa's side.

'Excuse me, may I get past?' he said. 'I'm from the CPS. You're not in the Grigg case, are you?'

'Only in a watching capacity.'

'Is that Mr Lidman?' he asked, nodding in the direction of the defending solicitor.

'Yes.'

'What on earth has he brought all those books for?' he asked in a worried tone. 'It's only a remand hearing.'

Rosa shrugged and gave him an ambivalent smile. She wasn't there to offer comfort to either side. She turned her head to scan the tiers of faces behind her, but saw nobody she recognised. She assumed the man sitting behind Lidman to be Grigg's cousin, Alex Cartwright. He wore an agitated look as he leaned forward and whispered keenly into the defending solicitor's ear. Lidman listened for a while, then put up a hand as if to brush him away.

An usher called for silence and the magistrate entered. Ms Godstone was a tall woman with severely cut iron-grey hair which seemed to set the tone of her whole presence. She radiated authority and dignity and it was hard to think of her doing anything apart from participating in thc impartial administration of justice. One certainly couldn't imagine her running for a bus or peeling potatoes.

At a nod from the clerk of the court, Tam Grigg stepped into the dock. He glanced quickly about him before giving the magistrate an unfriendly look which she received with equanimity.

Rosa was intrigued. She had not come across Ms Godstone before. She was a recent appointment and had been culled from some legal backwater.

The clerk read out the charge and the CPS lawyer rose to his feet.

'I am asking for a remand in custody, your worship,'

he said. 'The police still have many enquiries to make and there is the possibility of additional charges at a later stage. I don't think I need add anything further.'

The ever-hopeful members of the press turned their attention to Frank Lidman, who more often than not provided them with good copy. The man from the CPS was a write-off as far as they were concerned. He seemed unaware that there was a public waiting to be fed juicy tidbits to ease their journeys home after a day spent in the office. Evening papers welcomed a good murder story to boost their sales.

The defence solicitor didn't wait for any invitation from the magistrate before springing to his feet.

'In the circumstances, your worship, I can't object to the application for a remand,' he said in a tone that implied it was taking a herd of elephants to hold him back, 'but there are matters my client would like the court to know about at the earliest opportunity. Mr Grigg returned to this country from France as soon as he knew the police wished to interview him and presented himself to Detective Chief Inspector Cain. He strenuously denies the charge and will fight it every inch of the way. He will also contest any further charges that may be brought.' He gave the CPS lawyer a withering glance. 'In my view, the very mention of such a possibility is irrelevant and prejudicial.'

He was about to continue when the clerk broke in. 'Mr Lidman, there has been no application for reporting restrictions to be lifted and yet I have the impression you might wish that course to be taken.'

The solicitor looked momentarily aghast.

'Most certainly,' he said. 'Thank you for reminding me.' Lifting his gaze to the graven figure of Ms Godstone, he went on, 'I would like to apply for the lifting of reporting restrictions, your worship. Retrospectively.'

'Very well,' the magistrate said in a deep voice that befitted her appearance.

The press, most of whom had been ignorant of the procedural hiccup, picked up their pens again.

Frank Lidman rested his hands on one of the tomes he had brought and prepared to go on.

'I heard the representative of the Crown Prosecution Service mention further enquiries that had to be made. If that was intended as a warning that the prosecution won't be ready to proceed within a reasonable time, I should like to issue my own warning that I will harry him at every opportunity. Let him clearly understand that!' He gave the prosecuting solicitor a contemptuous glance, which caused Rosa to reflect that the cameraderie of the legal profession was not always on display.

'Finally,' Lidman said, taking a deep breath and assuming a stern expression, 'I should like to refer to the publicity in this case which has preceded my client being charged . . .'

'Mr Lidman,' Ms Godstone broke in, 'I don't wish to hear you on that aspect.'

'But I have a right to speak and you, madam, have an obligation to listen,' Frank Lidman said sternly.

'You have no such generalised right and I am certainly under no obligation to listen to anything not relevant to the matter in hand, namely the question of a remand in custody. Are you applying for bail?'

'Yes.'

'Bail is refused,' the magistrate replied crisply. 'Anything further, Mr Lidman? Otherwise I must ask you to resume your seat.'

With a final indignant splutter, the defence solicitor sank to his seat and Rosa looked at Ms Godstone with fresh respect. Anyone who could handle Frank Lidman so firmly and effectively deserved it.

A minute later the hearing was over and Grigg had been remanded in custody. As Rosa pushed her way out of court, Cain came up beside her.

'Good morning, Miss Epton. Are you here professionally or taking a busman's holiday?' he asked with a quizzical smile.

157

'I'm not really sure which,' Rosa replied with a small laugh.

'If you can spare a few minutes, I'd like to talk to you. There's a café round the corner where we can get a cup of coffee.' He glanced about him. 'Sergeant Saddler can deal with the aftermath here. I'll just tell him where we'll be. That is, if you're agreeable?'

'Yes, that's fine,' she said, intrigued to find out what Cain had to say.

'Good. I'll join you there in a couple of minutes.'

Rosa found the café and sat down at a table. She had barely had time to take in her surroundings when Cain arrived.

'Do you mind if we move to that table at the back? There'll be less chance of the press spotting us.' He went to the counter and returned with two cups of *cappuccino*. 'The magistrate really put Frank Lidman in his place, didn't she? She not only looks the part, but plays it as well.'

'Wait till the police get on the wrong side of her. You may change your view.'

'I know what you mean, but, in fact, if the police ever did deserve a roasting, she'd have my backing.'

He sipped the froth on top of his coffee. Watching him, Rosa had the feeling that though he was outwardly his calm, laid-back self, beneath the surface lay a build-up of tension. It showed in his eyes.

'You must be glad to have made an arrest,' she remarked. 'I imagine the pressure's been on from the word go.'

'You can say that again,' he replied with a weary sigh. 'Not only has been, but still is. And will be until someone has been convicted of Eddie Ruding's murder.'

'Someone?'

He glanced up from stirring his coffee and said, 'Do you believe it was Grigg?'

'I don't know what evidence you have,' Rosa said cautiously.

'Oh, there's evidence all right. Mostly circumstantial, but

158

none the worse for that. He wouldn't have been charged if there hadn't been evidence.' He gave Rosa a wry smile. 'The CPS gave the go-ahead, albeit a trifle nervously, so the police are covered. For police, read Richard Cain,' he added drily.

'So what's troubling you?'

'Somehow it doesn't feel right. Do you know what I mean?' Rosa nodded and he went on, 'It's like a jigsaw puzzle where certain pieces which don't really fit have been forced into position.'

'Mrs Ruding is quite certain Grigg killed her son and Joe Gillfroy was equally sure.'

'I know. As to Gillfroy's death, we can prove a motive of sorts against Grigg. Joe was shouting the odds too loudly and ignored the warning to shut his mouth. But I'm still at a loss to find a motive for Eddie's death.'

'Grigg hasn't said anything that helps, in the course of your interviews with him?'

'Not a thing.'

'He and Eddie seem to have known one another quite well.' Cain nodded and Rosa went on, 'Is there any evidence that Grigg is a pervert?'

Cain looked at her in surprise. 'A sexual pervert, do you mean?'

'It's just that, in my view, there's something sadistic about both murders.'

'I suppose there was,' Cain said in a thoughtful tone. 'Cruel, at any rate. The method was cold-blooded and depositing Joe's body on top of Eddie's grave was particularly nasty. But it is scarcely evidence of sexual perversion.'

'Isn't it a fact that every perversion has a sexual connotation?'

'I wouldn't know.'

'I was speaking to Clive Fox just before I went into court and he averred that he could find a sexual interest in every murder case if he searched hard enough.'

159

Cain laughed. 'I'm sure he could. It helps to sell his newspaper.'

A silence fell and Rosa finished her coffee. Then, pushing her cup and saucer away, she said, 'I'm still waiting to hear why you wanted to talk to me. I've enjoyed my cup of coffee and talking about the case, but I'd assumed there was something specific you wanted to discuss.' She gave him an encouraging smile. 'Am I right? Or maybe you're having second thoughts?'

For a while he stared into his empty cup, apparently marshalling his thoughts. When he spoke, his words took Rosa completely by surprise.

'I understand you met Colin Kirby at Pierre's Bar a few evenings ago,' he said. 'Would I be right in thinking that was at Kirby's suggestion? If you tell me to mind my own business, I'll have to accept your answer, but I hope you won't say that.'

It was Rosa's turn to become thoughtful while she pondered the question. Or not so much the question as its implications.

'May I ask how you know that we met? Did Kirby tell you?'

Cain shook his head. 'Kirby is wholly unaware of our knowledge of the meeting.'

'Then either he or I must be under surveillance.'

'I assure you that you are not. May I just say that you were seen there together? I'd sooner not explain further, though I promise you I'm not setting a trap or trying to get you to incriminate yourself in any way.' He gave her a disarming smile. 'I hope you know me well enough to accept that.'

Nevertheless, he is still a policeman, Rosa reflected, though in this instance we're not on opposite sides. And yes, I do trust him not to land me in difficulty.

'You're right in thinking we met at Kirby's suggestion,' she said with a deprecating gesture. 'He phoned me earlier in the day and asked if we could meet. I agreed, more out

160

of curiosity than anything else, and he proposed we should do so at Pierre's Bar.' Cain waited for her to continue. 'It sounds extraordinary, but what he wanted me to do was to write to his bosses expressing my conviction of his innocence. It still sounds absurd, but that's what he said. He knew he'd come under suspicion in connection with Ruding's death and was anxious to rehabilitate himself. He purported to believe I could help him.'

'What was your reaction?'

'I told him bluntly I didn't see that anything I could say would be of any assistance. Quite frankly, I was completely nonplussed by his request. It struck me as being devoid of any reality.'

'You turned him down flat, in fact?'

'I said I'd think over what he'd told me, but made it clear I was unlikely to change my mind.'

'Did you part amicably?'

'Let's say, politely. I've never taken to him and I still remember how unhelpful he was when Ruding was awaiting trial. Indeed, until we met at Pierre's Bar our relationship might be said to have existed in permafrost. He did his best – at least, I assume it was his best – to unthaw it over a drink, but I can't pretend he was very successful.'

Cain nodded slowly. 'Did he say anything at all about Ruding's murder?'

'Nothing, except to deny his guilt. He said it was preposterous to think of him as a murderer. In fact, he seemed genuinely indignant that he'd fallen under suspicion.'

'You must have been surprised that he wanted to meet you and even more so when you learnt the reason?'

'I was and still am.'

'But you didn't have any hesitation in agreeing to meet him?'

Rosa frowned. Cain's last two questions sounded very much like cross-examination.

'I've told you that I went purely out of curiosity,' she said in a nettled tone.

161

He held up a placatory hand. 'I'm sorry. I'm only trying to clarify my own mind. Has he been in touch with you since then?'

'No.'

'And you've not spoken to him?'

'No.'

'Did he appear quite normal when you met?'

Rosa pulled a face. 'By his own standards, yes. He's always struck me as a somewhat graceless person. But probably smooth talk and graciousness weren't highly rated qualities in the ex-Rhodesian Police.'

'Or in a good many other police forces for that matter,' Cain added with a grin. He paused for a moment. 'One of the reasons I wanted to talk to you, Miss Epton, is that Kirby has disappeared.'

Chapter 23

So that was it. That was why he had wanted to talk to her. He believed that her meeting with Kirby was connected with his disappearance.

After this bare announcement, Cain had gone to the counter to fetch two further cups of coffee. He now turned to come back, walking with concentrated determination not to spill the cups' contents.

'Yes, he disappeared a few days ago. A day or so after you met him, though I was only informed yesterday. I take it he didn't say anything to you about going away?'

'Nothing.'

'He didn't mention a vacation?' Rosa shook her head and Cain smothered a yawn. 'I'm afraid I didn't get a great deal of sleep last night. Grigg, Kirby and my pregnant wife all saw to that. As to Kirby, he applied for ten days' leave which was granted, after his boss had phoned me to ask if there was any police objection. I felt obliged to say no. I knew he would leave an address where he could be contacted, if necessary. It seems that, for one reason and another, he'd not taken leave for some time and had an accumulation. He later told his people he had booked in at a small hotel at a fishing village on the west coast of Scotland. He intended taking a night train to Glasgow and hiring a car. So, having obtained everyone's blessing, he set off. Or, to be accurate, he left home.

'Two days later, his boss decided to phone him, just to check he had gone where he said. He had phoned earlier and confirmed that Kirby had, indeed, made a reservation at the hotel. When he called the second time, however, he was informed that Kirby hadn't shown up, nor had he cancelled his reservation and he owed them money. Discreet enquiries were made at British Rail and it was discovered he had not used the sleeper he'd reserved. At that point alarm bells began to ring and I was informed.' He gave Rosa a rueful look. 'End of story.'

'There could be a perfectly innocent explanation,' Rosa said tentatively.

'That he's suffering from loss of memory, for example?'

'It's a possibility. He must have been under an enormous strain these past few weeks.'

'Colin Kirby is a tough, resilient animal.'

'Even so, he must have a breaking point. Is it known what he took with him when he went away?'

'As a matter of fact, we gained entry to his flat yesterday evening. There was no sign of a panic dash and nothing of an incriminating nature. Also his Volvo estate is still parked outside.'

'There was nothing connecting him with Eddie Ruding?'

'No.' He gave Rosa a wry look. 'I'm more concerned with strengthening the case against Grigg than having it proved I've arrested the wrong person.'

After several minutes of frowning thought, Rosa said, 'How's this as a scenario for Kirby's disappearance? He's always been a loner and someone prepared to use his initiative, even if it meant breaking the rules. He's clearly obsessed with rehabilitating himself in MI5. That much emerged at my meeting with him. Isn't it possible that is precisely what he has gone off to do? He's realised nobody else is likely to help him and he's decided to show you and his colleagues what a rotten bunch you are. When he reappears it will be to bring you proof positive that he's a much maligned person.'

'How will he be able to do that?' Cain enquired in a tone of considerable suspicion.

'I don't know how, but of one thing I am sure: Kirby is the one person who can fill all the gaps in the case.'

'Of course, if he has vanished for good, Grigg's certain to be acquitted. The defence will be able to pin everything on Kirby, last heard of in an African jungle.'

'He'll reappear.'

'What makes you say that?'

'Feminine intuition.'

'Nothing more substantial than that?'

'It's the best I can offer you at the moment.'

Chapter 24

Vincent Ruding had bought time. How much remained to be seen, but for the moment the pressure had been eased. This wasn't out of kindness or consideration on the part of those who had been threatening him. The threat was still there. Unspecified, but predictably disagreeable.

'We're prepared to offer you a deal,' the familiar voice had said on the phone.

'What sort of deal?' Ruding had enquired nervously.

'Meet me at the Café Benedict across from the Central station at eight o'clock this evening.'

'Could you make it a bit later . . . ?'

'No,' the voice cut in. 'Eight o'clock and don't be late or you'll get something less friendly than the offer of a deal.'

The man was already there when Ruding arrived. He was sitting at a table with a glass of schnapps in front of him.

'Go and buy yourself a drink if you want one,' he said.

Ruding went to the bar and returned with a glass of beer.

'Do you know Colin Kirby?'

'The MI5 chap?'

'Yes,' the man said with a touch of impatience.

'I don't know him well.'

'But he knows who you are and that you're Eddie Ruding's brother?'

'Yes.'

'Good enough. We want to have a talk to him.'

'You don't need me for that.'

'That's where you're wrong. We want you to get him to Amsterdam.'

'How can I do that?' Ruding asked anxiously. 'I've told you I hardly know him. He's not going to come here just because I tell him to.'

'Finished? Good, then listen. You'll phone him at his home and say that you've found out something about Eddie which you feel he should know. Which he'll want to know. You'll say it's too sensitive to mention over an open telephone line and that as you're unable to leave Amsterdam, he must come over and visit you.'

'He's never going to accept all that. He'll think it's a trap.'

'It's up to you to make it plausible. If he refuses to come, we shan't have a deal and that won't be good for you.'

'When do you want me to call him?'

'This evening. I'll give you his home number.'

'It can't possibly work.'

'You may be in for a surprise. I hope so for your sake.'

'Supposing he just hangs up?'

165

'Then you call him again immediately and ask him if he's seen Dieter recently.'

'Dieter? Who's Dieter?'

'It doesn't matter who Dieter is. Kirby'll know who you are talking about.'

'And?'

'I think you'll find he'll agree to come over. He may even be on the next plane.'

'What am I to do when he arrives?'

'Tell him to call you from the airport.'

That had been a few days earlier and Colin Kirby was now at Schipol airport looking at the piece of paper on which he had noted Vincent Ruding's telephone number.

In one sense, things could not have worked out more conveniently. He had been granted leave and had made arrangements to go to Scotland. It was a simple matter to switch to Holland. He had no intention of notifying anyone of his change of plan, especially not his department, which would have shown unwanted curiosity. He would cope with the aftermath of his changed plans when he saw what form it took.

He walked unhurriedly across to a payphone and rang Ruding's number.

'Ruding? It's Kirby,' he said when he recognised the voice that answered.

'Oh, hello, glad you've come. Where are you?'

Ruding sounded nervous, which increased Kirby's suspicion.

'At the airport.'

'Well, jump into a taxi and come along to Jutenberger-straat. I'll expect you in about thirty minutes.'

You'll be lucky, Kirby thought. I'll come when I feel like it and not a minute before.

When he received Ruding's call, he had naturally wondered if he was being set up. And if so, by whom and for what purpose? Whoever had put Ruding up to making

166

the call had clearly not rehearsed him sufficiently. He had sounded awkward and ill at ease. Nevertheless, it was probable that curiosity would have brought him across the North Sea anyway. But the cryptic mention of Dieter had put his decision beyond doubt. What did Ruding know about Dieter? Almost certainly nothing, but somebody else did. The somebody who had devised the scheme to get him to Amsterdam. He had packed a bag and left home immediately, though it wasn't until two days later he flew to Holland.

Turning his back on the telephone, he walked over to a bar and ordered a beer. It was two o'clock in the afternoon and he was in no hurry to move.

While he was drinking the beer he pulled a street plan of Amsterdam from his pocket and looked for Jutenbergerstraat. He wanted to familiarise himself with the area. A good intelligence officer is one who is well briefed.

Half an hour later he strolled out of the airport terminal and got into a taxi. He told the driver to take him to the Rijksmuseum. He didn't propose visiting its collection of Rembrandts, but it was a convenient landmark on the fringe of the inner city from which to make his next move. There was also a hotel near by where he had once stayed and where he would leave his bag. He would book in for the night if they had a room.

The hotel receptionist told him he was in luck as they had just had a cancellation. Otherwise they were fully booked. He accepted the information with a curt nod. If the receptionist had been expecting profuse thanks, he could go on expecting.

Seventy-five minutes had passed since he had called Ruding from the airport. He decided to wait another three-quarters of an hour before making his next move. On occasions such as this, it was a sound principle to keep people waiting, to appear relaxed but wary, and to hang on to the initiative for as long as possible. He certainly didn't want it to appear that it was the mention of Dieter that had

167

brought him to the city. Dieter was a bad memory.

A taxi dropped him in Jutenbergerstraat and he walked slowly toward the block where Vincent Ruding was employed as a caretaker. Several times he paused and glanced casually about him. Eventually he reached his destination and rang the bell. There was a buzz and a click and the street door sprang open a few inches. The entryphone remained silent. He ran quietly down the stairs to the basement. The door of Ruding's flat was closed and no sound came from the further side. For several seconds he stood on the bottom step and waited. Then bracing himself, he walked quickly across and rang the bell, standing to one side so as not to present a target.

The door was opened with a suddenness that told him he was dealing with a professional like himself. The man who confronted him was not Vincent Ruding.

'Come in,' the man said. 'We thought you must have got lost.'

'Where's Ruding?' Kirby asked as he stepped cautiously inside.

'He had to go out.'

'Give us a kiss,' said the parrot.

Kirby ignored it. He hadn't come to exchange small talk with a parrot.

Vincent Ruding's instructions were to go away and not return for at least three hours. When he did come back, he was to ring the doorbell and go away again if so informed on the entryphone.

The man he had previously met was accompanied by a smaller man who had cold, grey eyes and wore rimless spectacles. No introductions were made, but it was clear that the new man was the senior of the two.

After leaving them in possession of his flat to await Kirby's arrival, Ruding took a tram and got off in Leidsestraat. He walked slowly in the direction of the old city centre, staring into shop windows as he went. His mind, however, was on other things; chiefly his brother's death and the problems it had brought. He had read of Tam Grigg's arrest and wondered if the police would be able to pin the other murder on him as well. Meanwhile, it was always good news when someone like Grigg was kept out of circulation. And if it kept the police quiet, so much the better.

It was in the course of a morose train of thought that something occurred to him. Why shouldn't he waylay Kirby as he left the flat and ask him for the money he was being pressed to pay? Admittedly, the pressure had eased, but that might be only temporary, and this was an opportunity worth exploiting. He was reasonably sure that the three men wouldn't depart together and that Kirby was likely to be the first to leave.

So thinking, he turned on his heel and made his way back to Jutenbergerstraat. There was a bar not far from his block where he was known and where he could sit outside at one of the pavement tables and observe all the comings and goings.

He had been sitting there for over an hour before he saw Kirby leave the building and start walking in his direction. He was moving with a purposeful stride as if to put immediate distance between himself and the flat. Ruding waited until he was almost directly on the opposite pavement before getting up and hurrying after his quarry. He reached the further pavement with Kirby ten yards ahead and gaining ground.

'Mr Kirby,' he called out as he broke into a run.

Kirby halted in his tracks and looked round, giving Ruding a chance to catch him up.

'I don't like having my name shouted out like that,' he said angrily.

'I'm sorry, but I need to speak to you.'

'What about?' Kirby's tone was anything but friendly.

'The money my brother took from Bilak's flat. I'm being pressed to hand it over to the men you met at my flat.'

'Then I advise you to do so, before they turn you into

169

food for police dogs.' Ruding gave him a startled look and Kirby went on, 'It'd be no more than you deserve. After all, it was you who murdered your brother.'

Kirby caught a plane first thing the next morning. The Special Branch officer who examined his passport at Heathrow did a quick double-take when he saw the name, but returned it without comment.

So they know I didn't go to Scotland, he thought as he made his way to the Underground. He had always realised they might check on his movements and he was glad that the officer in question had given himself away. He now knew where he stood.

An hour later he arrived at his flat and let himself in. To someone as experienced as himself in the field of exploring other people's homes without leaving a trace, it was immediately obvious there had been intruders during his absence. Throwing his bag on the bed, he picked up the phone and rang his headquarters. Decker's secretary answered and he asked to be put through to the man who was his superior officer for most purposes.

'Hello, Colin,' Decker said with his customary urbanity. 'Where are you calling from?'

'Home. I'm afraid I never got to Scotland.'

'So where have you been?'

'I think it would be best if I came into the office and explained.'

'Certainly. I understand somebody did try and get in touch with you at the address you gave, but the hotel said you'd not turned up.'

Kirby was not taken in by Decker's apparently casual manner. Drama and histrionics were alien to his nature.

'I'll come straightaway.'

'Good. Look forward to seeing you.'

So far, so good, Kirby reflected as he sat in a taxi taking him to headquarters. He knew, however, that a reprimand was the least he could expect. And with his career already in question that was not something to be welcomed.

'Come in and sit down,' Decker said, when Kirby entered his office. A man named Smedley from Establishments was with him. 'You'd better start at the beginning.'

'You remember Bilak, the man whose flat Ruding burgled?' Decker gave a brief nod to indicate that the question was superfluous. 'Well, the day before I was going up to Scotland, I received information that Bilak was now in Holland. In Amsterdam to be precise. I was keen to confirm the truth of this and decided to go over and check. So I scrapped my holiday plans and flew to Amsterdam yesterday morning. I'd been told where Bilak was living and went straight to his address. Unfortunately, he had left the previous day. I then realised I had acted impetuously and decided I'd better return and tell you where I'd been and why.' He paused and went on in the gruff tone that passed for contrition, 'I've been desperately worried about my career ever since the Ruding débâcle and my one and only concern has been to rehabilitate myself in the eyes of the service. I've been a hard-working officer who's not been afraid to use his initiative. I know that has sometimes led me to bend the rules, but nobody's complained as long as I produced the goods.' He smiled sourly. 'Unfortunately, the Bilak affair has been one disaster leading to another. I'm sorry for all the trouble I've caused, but I ask you to accept that I've acted from the best of motives, namely to try and put right what went wrong.'

'That all you want to say?' Decker said. Kirby nodded and Decker went on, 'As to your motives, it seems to me you've acted out of pure self-interest. Your only concern has been to restore our confidence and a fine mess you've made of that. Initiative is one thing; trying to play all the instruments in the band yourself is the height of folly.

'You'd better go away and write a full report, setting out everything you've said and answering the more obvious questions your conduct gives rise to.' Observing Kirby's expression, he added, 'Such as, your source of information

171

that Bilak was in Amsterdam.' He paused. 'And don't leave the building until you've done it, Colin.'

'He's more trouble than he's worth,' the man from Establishments said, after Kirby had left the room.

'Yes and no,' Decker remarked. 'He's certainly a rotten PR man in his own cause.' He gazed out of the window. 'I'd better let Cain know the position. His own grapevine may have told him, but I wouldn't want him to waste time on enquiries when we have Kirby tucked away in our own building. Incidentally, you'd better inform our security people that he's not to leave without specific authority. I don't suppose he'd try, but with Colin Kirby one can't be too sure of anything.'

Chapter 25

Frank Lidman was not looking forward to visiting his client in prison. It was five days since the court had remanded him in custody and one day since a High Court judge sitting in chambers had turned down his application for bail. Lidman had warned him that the chances of a successful application were slim, but Grigg had insisted that every step be taken to get him bail.

By now, he would have been informed of the judge's decision, but that wasn't going to make Lidman's visit any easier. It was one of the times when the solicitor looked forward to retirement to the apartment he and his wife had bought at Palm Beach, Florida. It was a prospect that became increasingly appealing as his clients seemed to become ever more demanding and tiresome. Admittedly they paid heavily for his professional services, but what was the point of making money if you never had proper time to enjoy it? There was also the risk factor. His clients paid over the odds because they expected him to take risks on their behalf. They didn't want to be told that the law was not in their favour. To Grigg, and many others, the law was there to be manipulated, circumvented and generally left bleeding on the battlefield. Lidman had reached the point where he was tired of taking risks on behalf of a bunch of men whose only attraction was their ability to pay his exorbitant charges.

These were his predominant thoughts as he drove to the prison that afternoon. He enjoyed the admiring glances his Rolls-Royce received, happily oblivious to the fact that they were often glances of amusement at the incongruous sight of the gleaming, luxurious car and the funny bald-headed little man crouched behind the steering-wheel.

As he sat in the lawyers' interview room waiting for Grigg, he had virtually made up his mind to give up practice and retire at the end of the present year. He knew that his wife, Bernice, would be delighted. He would put their house in Finchley on the market and ship the Rolls out to Florida before they left. There it would grace the palm-fringed boulevards and be a valuable status symbol.

A door opened and Grigg appeared. Being on remand, he was still wearing his own clothes. Prison garb was for those serving sentences after conviction.

Lidman gave his client a cautious smile. 'Sorry about the bail application, Tam, but I did warn you that it probably wouldn't succeed.'

'So what's the next step to get me out of here?'

'We can renew the application next time you appear in the magistrates' court.'

Grigg gave his solicitor an impatient look.

'That's not what I meant.'

'What did you mean, Tam?' Lidman asked, with a sinking feeling.

'I want you to get me out of this place by one means or another.'

The solicitor sighed. 'These things take time to arrange.'

'They need not.'

'And cost money.'

'No problem.'

'And can end in disaster.'

'Nothing venture, nothing lose. But it won't end in disaster if it's properly planned.' Grigg lowered his voice. 'There's a prison officer on my wing who'll help if it's made worth his while. I want you to visit him at his home and take a couple of thousand pounds with you. He'll tell you what to do. With a getaway car waiting, I could be out of the country in a couple of hours.'

'You're asking me to take a colossal risk.'

'And paying you as well.'

'Give me a day to think about it.'

Grigg shook his head. 'I'm not asking you a favour, Frank. I'm giving you an instruction.'

Lidman bridled at the audacity of the threat. 'The fact that you are where you are is your own bloody fault. It was your decision to come home and walk into Scotland Yard. Of all the daft things you've ever done . . .'

'Shut your mouth, Frank. When I want your opinion, I'll tell you. Meanwhile, just bear in mind that homely saying about the person who pays the piper calls the tune. I'm the one paying the piper and I'm telling you the tune. Now, here's the name and address of the prison officer you're to visit. But make sure you phone him first.'

Lidman glanced at the slip of paper with distaste. Grigg seemed to read his thoughts for he went on, 'And don't get any funny ideas, Frank. Just remember that I have enough on you to have you struck off. Isn't that the correct expression? If necessary, I'll have you struck out and struck down as well. Just remember that. Come and see me again in a couple of days.'

It was a thoughtful Frank Lidman who returned to his car. Palm Beach seemed more attractive than ever. One had to be crazy to put up with a megalomaniac client like Tam Grigg.

As for the present case, he hadn't yet addressed his

174

mind to the question of Grigg's guilt. He had listened to his client's angry protestations of innocence, but that was all. He accepted that most of his clients were guilty, though that was never a factor which inhibited his efforts in their defence.

As he drove back to his office, which was situated in one of Mayfair's less populous streets, he wondered who *had* murdered Joe Gillfroy (also Eddie Ruding, for that matter) if it wasn't his client? He had better start giving it thought.

His solicitor was not the only person to be put under pressure by Grigg. Alex Cartwright found himself expected to pay a daily visit to the prison and to perform the combined duties of secretary, courier and general dogsbody. It was a role to which he had become inured. Tam was the boss and he was the loyal assistant. He enjoyed the fruits of crime, but not the life; and without the fruits he had no hope of keeping Shirley happy. She was one of the great spenders. As for Tam, Alex reckoned he must have several hundred thousand stashed away in foreign bank accounts, not that it was something he ever talked about.

It was in a reflective frame of mind that Cartwright arrived at the prison on the afternoon following Lidman's visit.

Grigg and Cartwright sat opposite each other at a table with cups of tea and chocolate biscuits in front of them. Children scampered around the tables while their mothers sat in huddled conversation with their menfolk. A small girl paused beside Grigg and stared at him wide-eyed until he told her to buzz off.

'Frank was here yesterday,' Tam said. 'Has he been in touch?'

'Not yet.'

'Well, he should have been.' He lowered his voice. 'I gave him the particulars of a friendly screw. I want you to liaise with Frank about the details. Know what I mean? I'm not going to spend an hour longer in this place than I have to.' He glanced about him with an expression of deep distaste.

Refocusing his gaze on his cousin, he went on, 'You're one of the few people I can trust, Alex.' Then, 'I can still trust you, can't I, Alex?'

'Of course, Tam.'

'Good, because I'm not as confident about Frank Lidman's loyalty as I'd like to be. Maybe he was out of sorts when he was here yesterday, but I don't pay him to be stroppy. He'd better remember who has the whip-hand.' He gave Alex a sour smile. 'There are others who'd be leading healthier lives if they'd remembered that.' He smothered a yawn. 'Bring me some indigestion tablets when you come tomorrow. The food here would disgrace a pig's trough.'

That same afternoon Rosa didn't return to the office until after six o'clock. She had been in court the whole afternoon and had gone from there to the Temple for a conference with counsel. Normally, she wouldn't have bothered to return, but there were some papers she needed to work on before a morning in court the next day.

She thought it possible that she would find Robin in his office as he often preferred to stay late rather than take work home. But the building was silent and deserted. She let herself in and went along to her room to fetch what she needed.

It was customary for Stephanie to switch on the answering machine before she went home in the evening and Rosa decided to find out if there were any messages for her. She pressed the replay switch and listened. The machine hummed for a couple of seconds, then let out a small hiccup, before a vaguely familiar voice began speaking.

'Message for solicitor Epton,' it said. 'Ask Colin Kirby if he's seen Dieter recently. That's all.'

It ended with a strange inarticulate sound. Considerably perplexed, Rosa decided to play it back and listen even more carefully. She was still trying to pinpoint the voice in her memory when the message reached its end and she realised that the final curious noise was a parrot's squawk.

Chapter 26

Rosa drove home in a thoughtful mood. The first thing she did on arrival was to open windows and get a current of air flowing through her flat, which became an oven in summer when it was shut up all day. Next she poured herself a glass of chilled white wine. She stood sipping it in the kitchen while she decided what to have for supper. Eventually, with her mind still not made up, she took her drink into the living-room. Perhaps later she would make an omelette, but it could wait, for she realised she wasn't really very hungry. She put on a Nat King Cole tape and sat down to listen and think. If Peter were at home she would have called him, but he had flown to Rome that morning on business and wouldn't be home until the next evening at the earliest.

The strange message on the answering machine had left her feeling that she ought to do something. Now.

It was no good calling Robin as she knew what his advice would be. Inform the police and do nothing on her own account. And that wasn't what she wanted to hear.

She looked at her watch. It was just after seven thirty and she returned to the kitchen to pour herself another glass of wine. She took some salad ingredients from the refrigerator as a start toward her supper, but her mind was still on the message she had received. She would eventually have identified Vincent Ruding's voice, but the parrot had saved her the trouble.

She suddenly decided to call him and wondered why it had taken her so long to reach that decision.

A woman answered the phone and a torrent of incomprehensible words followed Rosa's request to speak to Vincent Ruding. She heard a door slam and then his voice came on the line. He said something in Dutch before Rosa could speak.

'Is that Vincent Ruding?' she asked.

'Who is that?'

'Rosa Epton. You called my office and left a message.'

'I think you have a wrong number. It's a bad line.'

Make up your mind, Rosa thought, as she tried to conceal her impatience.

'I can hear you quite clearly,' she said. 'I'm calling about the message you left on my office answering machine. What exactly does it mean?'

There was a lengthy silence before he spoke. Rosa wondered if, perhaps, he had not expected her to recognise his voice and was taken aback by her call. In that case he had reckoned without his parrot.

'It means what it says,' he said in an off-hand way.

'Who is Dieter?'

Rosa heard him sigh. 'I've no idea.' Then with seeming reluctance, he added, 'All I know is that Kirby comes running if you mention it to him.' After a further pause, he went on, 'I suppose I'd better explain . . .'

'So that's where Kirby disappeared to,' Rosa remarked when Ruding had finished. 'Is he still in Amsterdam?'

'I can't tell you. He's not been in touch with me.'

'And you have no idea who this Dieter person is?'

'None.'

After ringing off, Rosa fell once more into deep thought. It now seemed possible that Kirby was a double agent and had been one all along. It could be that Eddie Ruding had rumbled the fact and been murdered as a consequence. The thought, however, that Joe Gillfroy had been mixed up in the world of espionage was too ludicrous for words.

For a few moments, she continued staring at the telephone. She had called Ruding. Why not now call Kirby on his home number which he had given her? If he answered, she would hang up without speaking. And then in the morning she would phone Cain and tell him what she had found out.

Picking up the receiver, she tapped out the digits of

178

his Pimlico number. Her heart began to beat faster while she waited. She had persuaded herself there would be no reply, so that when his unmistakable voice came down the line she almost gave herself away. Without a word, however, she dropped the receiver back into place.

She had been so certain that his phone would remain unanswered that she felt disorientated by the outcome of her call.

She ate her supper – a cheese omelette and a green salad with a French dressing – without really tasting it. Afterwards she made a cup of coffee and sat down by the open window to read the papers she had fetched from the office. But concentration didn't come readily and she found her mind constantly going off on tangents which had Colin Kirby and somebody called Dieter at their point of contact.

About ten o'clock she decided to call Kirby's number again. If he answered, she would say that she had been thinking about the letter he had asked her to write and did he still want her to do so? It sounded feeble, but at least gave her an excuse for phoning.

She half hoped there would be no reply, for then she could go to bed knowing she had tried to speak to him and had not funked the situation. If she took no action, she knew it would nag her into sleeplessness.

This time his telephone didn't ring more than twice before he answered.

'It's Rosa Epton. I hope I'm not disturbing you.'

'Go ahead. What's on your mind?' His tone was wary, as she had found it so often before.

'I did try and call you a few days ago, but I think you must have been away. Anyway, there was no answer.'

'You could have left a message on my machine.'

'I didn't think that would be very discreet in the circumstances.'

'You're right, it wouldn't have been. So what have you decided? About the letter, I mean?'

'I think it might be better if we met again and you told me precisely what you want. You could even bring me a draft I could use.'

'I thought solicitors usually drafted letters for other people, not the other way about.'

Rosa gave a nervous laugh. 'I agree, that is more customary. But this is rather a special letter and needs to be carefully tailored to your needs.'

'I'm obviously putting you to more trouble than I'd intended. Perhaps you'd best forget the whole thing. I know you weren't enthusiastic about writing it and . . . and, anyway, circumstances have changed.'

Rosa took a deep breath. 'Would Dieter have anything to do with that?'

'Who?' he asked after what seemed an interminable pause.

'Dieter.'

'I've no idea who you're talking about. Where did that name come from?'

'If you don't know him, it doesn't matter.'

'I'd still be interested to hear. I don't care for riddles.' He paused. 'Surely that's the least you can do; tell me where you got that name from.'

'I'm afraid I can't.'

'Have you been speaking to Cain?'

'No.'

'When was the last time?'

'I don't recall,' Rosa said, searching frantically for an excuse to ring off.

'You're not being very frank, Miss Epton. I thought better of you.'

'Look, I'm sorry I've troubled you. I have to go now.'

'Is your Chinese friend getting impatient?'

'Peter's not here, if that's what you're thinking. It's simply that I have to make an early start in the morning.'

'Goodnight, then.'

Rosa put down the telephone with relief and wiped her moist hand. It wasn't often she felt herself floundering, but her call to Kirby had had that effect. It was clear that the name Dieter did mean something to him, though what and why remained a mystery.

She went into her living-room and switched on the television, hoping for something anodyne to calm her seething mind. On one of the channels she found a 1930s Astaire–Rogers musical, which seemed the perfect answer. She watched it to the end. Dieter, Colin Kirby and Mrs Charlotte Ruding all fell into perspective under the magic of Fred and Ginger and Irving Berlin's music.

When the film was over, she spent half an hour reading the file she had brought home and was satisfied at the end that she was prepared for court the next morning.

She had hoped Peter might call her from Rome, though he had warned her it might not be possible. His client worked eccentric hours and expected his advisers to do likewise, which could mean conferring until the small hours of the morning.

'I hope you charge overtime,' Rosa had remarked.

'You bet,' Peter had replied. 'Triple time after midnight.'

Though they still had their separate flats, the nights they spent together were no longer confined to weekends. Rosa wished he was with her now.

She was feeling pleasantly sleepy by the time she got into bed, and she switched out the light immediately. It must have been an hour later, maybe more, when she woke up with a start. She had been having a vivid dream in which Mrs Ruding was chasing Tam Grigg across a field brandishing a hatchet. Rosa was shouting at her to stop, but she continued, gaining on Grigg all the while. He reached the bottom of the field and began clambering over a hedge, but she caught him up and struck him a ferocious blow with the hatchet. She then turned and came back to where Rosa was standing in horror.

'Serves the bastard right,' she remarked, slightly out of

breath. 'I've been wanting to do that for years. 'E killed my Eddie, now I've done 'im in. 'Ere, you take the 'atchet, you may need it.'

It was as she was proffering the blood-stained implement that Rosa woke up. For several seconds she lay still in the comforting reality of her own bed, her heart beats slowly returning to normal. She reached for the tumbler of water she always put on her bedside table and took three or four sips. She pressed the button that illuminated the face of her small alarm clock. It showed a few minutes after two o'clock. Turning onto her other side, she composed herself once more for sleep, hopeful that Mrs Ruding had been duly banished from any further dreams. But it was a warm, airless night and she feared that sleep wouldn't come easily a second time.

Twice she was about to drift off, but was awakened. The first time by a sudden tickle in her throat and the next by an invisible but persistent insect that seemed to be circling her head with a buzz as loud as a sawmill.

And then just as she was once more in the blissful state that precedes falling asleep, she was again disturbed. This time by a noise in the kitchen. Because it was a hot night she had left her bedroom door open and could therefore hear every sound throughout her small flat. She lifted her head from the pillow, but all was now silent. She decided that the noise had been caused by a sudden, welcome puff of air rattling something. Probably the half-lowered venetian blind. She lay quite still for several seconds, but heard nothing further. She took another sip of water, plumped up her pillow and lay back, resigned to the prospect of falling asleep just as it was time to get up.

It was not a noise so much as sixth sense that told her there was an intruder in the flat. He was standing in the bedroom doorway and she could see his dim outline in the light reflected from a street lamp.

This once happened to the Queen, she thought inconsequentially, but I don't have a panic button.

'Don't make a sound and don't move,' a voice said.

It was at the same time a relief and a cause for further alarm to find she recognised the speaker.

'What do you want?' she said with a mixture of fear and indignation. 'You must be mad breaking into my flat like this.'

The man advanced into the room and stood staring down at her.

'I want to hear exactly what you know about Dieter,' Colin Kirby said in a chilling tone, as he moved another step closer to the bed.

Chapter 27

He is mad, Rosa thought, as she stared back at him in the semi-darkness of her bedroom. I must try and calm him and gain his confidence, even if it's not an easy thing to do when you're lying flat on your back with a maniac standing over you.

'I don't know anything about Dieter,' she said helplessly, 'and that's the truth.'

'Where did you get his name from?'

'From Eddie's brother.'

'So! How did that come about?'

'He phoned my office and left a message suggesting I should ask you whether you'd seen Dieter recently.'

'What else?'

'That was all.'

'Didn't you call him back?'

Rosa hesitated. 'As a matter of fact, I did.'

'Go on.'

'He professed to knowing nothing about Dieter, either, but said he'd been instructed to use the name as a sort of code-word.' There was something particularly menacing about the stillness of the figure standing at her bedside. Haltingly, she went on, 'I was naturally curious. That's why I called you this evening.'

'You're Cain's fifth column, aren't you? That's really why you called me.'

'That's not true.'

'Of course it's true. It's why I had to come round immediately before you could speak to Cain in the morning.'

Rosa swallowed hard and tried to hide her mounting panic.

'Look, if you go now, I won't say anything to the police.'

'You know you can't wait to get on the phone,' he said scornfully, then went on in an almost casual tone, 'Do you believe I murdered Ruding?'

'Somebody's already been charged. Or, rather, charged with Joe Gillfroy's murder.'

'And you believe the same person committed both crimes?'

'It looks like it.'

'I agree. It looks very like it.' He paused. 'But you haven't answered my question. Do you believe I murdered Ruding?'

'As far as I know, you didn't have a motive,' Rosa said tensely.

'That's right, I didn't have a motive, so it couldn't have been me.'

Rosa chose this moment to scream. It was a long time since she had last screamed, but this proved no handicap. It was a scream to waken a whole neighbourhood and its effect on Kirby was electrifying. He vanished from the room and a few seconds later, Rosa heard the dying clatter of his departure down the fire escape.

Chief Inspector Cain arrived at Rosa's flat at four thirty that morning. She had phoned a duty officer at Scotland Yard within minutes of Kirby's departure and had impressed on him the need to contact Cain without delay.

'He'll know I wouldn't be calling at this hour of the night unless it were urgent,' she had said. 'Tell him that Colin Kirby broke into my flat and has just fled.'

The message had been sufficient and Cain had arrived within the hour. He was wearing a T-shirt and a pair of slacks. Rosa, for her part, had done her hair and put on a kimono (a present Peter had brought back from a trip to Tokyo).

As soon as he arrived she made a large pot of coffee, which she thought they would both need.

'Let's sit here at the kitchen table,' Cain said.

'There are more comfortable chairs in the living-room.'

'I know. That's why it would be better to stay here.'

He listened without interruption while Rosa related the evening's events, beginning with Vincent Ruding's message.

'I imagine you know who Dieter is,' she said, as she reached the end of her recital.

'I've no idea, but I'll certainly find out soon enough. The first move will be to detain Kirby. May I use your phone?'

He spent the next five minutes talking to someone at the Yard called Rob and to a duty officer at MI5. The latter call produced a return one from Decker, who was ringing from his home near Dorking.

'Is there any more coffee in that pot, Miss Epton?' he said when he had made his calls and Decker had promised to drive up to town immediately. 'Now that I've put everything in train, I should like to hear your theory about Kirby.'

'You remember that piece of paper I found in one of Joe Gillfroy's pockets, the piece with figures and dates on it?' Cain nodded and Rosa went on, 'The dates were all subsequent to Eddie's death and I reckoned the figures represented sums of money. Money that Joe had been paid for some service—'

'Or as a result of blackmail,' Cain broke in.

185

'I thought of blackmail, but the amounts seemed so paltry. It suddenly struck me, however, that Joe never lost an opportunity to suggest Grigg was a murderer. It was either a genuine belief or he was being paid to peddle that particular line. You remember how he was arrested for loitering near a jeweller's shop which Grigg had acquired for money-laundering purposes? His story to me was that he was hoping to find further evidence against Grigg. At the time I thought he was acting out of genuine conviction and loyalty toward his dead friend. Even so I was troubled, for Joe hadn't struck me as a person capable of strong personal loyalty nor as someone driven by conviction. I began to wonder if he was acting a part. If he was, the only person interested in deflecting suspicion away from himself was Eddie's murderer.'

'And you believe that was Kirby?' Cain said. Rosa nodded and he went on, 'It now looks very much as if Kirby may have been a double agent – at least, that's MI5's fear – and that Eddie Ruding rumbled the fact.'

'I think Eddie rumbled something else,' Rosa said. 'Something which led him to blackmail Kirby.' Cain looked at her with a puzzled expression. 'Unless I'm very much mistaken, Colin Kirby is a homosexual,' she said.

'He can't be,' Cain exclaimed. 'He's been through all the vetting procedures and they'd have found out.' Rosa gave him a sardonic glance and his shoulders sagged. 'I know people can slip through the net, but Kirby always seemed particularly macho.'

'Not all homosexuals have limp wrists and a camp gait.'

'I'm aware of that. But Kirby . . . Anyway, what's the basis for your allegation?'

'I'm pretty sure Eddie Ruding was one,' Rosa said. 'I'm not suggesting they ever had a relationship and very possibly they didn't, but, as they say, it takes one to recognise one. Eddie felt bitter and thoroughly let down over the Bilak affair, even though Kirby subsequently pulled out all the stops to get him released. I recall Joe telling me the first

186

time we met that Eddie had got himself a nice little meal ticket and I thought at the time he could be referring to blackmail. It's my belief he began blackmailing Kirby almost as soon as he was out of prison.'

'Where does his visit to Amsterdam fit in?'

'My guess would be that Bilak's friends had ideas about using Eddie and made an approach. Remember that Eddie was a born opportunist.'

'That's all very well, Miss Epton, but you've still not told me why you believe Kirby is homosexual.'

Rosa gave him a deprecating smile. 'You know the way they're always seeking to make eye contact with others of similar taste? It's part of their courting procedure. Well, when I met Kirby at Pierre's Bar, there was a young waiter he couldn't keep his eyes off. He was like a Rottweiler being tempted by a T-bone steak. It was only later that the full impact of the situation struck me. At the time I was too busy trying to make sense of our meeting.'

'And what sense did you make of it?'

'I think he genuinely hoped I'd write the sort of letter he wanted and that it would assist in his rehabilitation.'

'Some hope!'

'I agree.'

'He must be mad.'

'I agree again.'

'I don't mean insane in law,' Cain said quickly.

'Probably not, but still a sadistic pervert,' Rosa remarked. 'Killing people with karate chops to their necks and depositing their bodies in bizarre places obviously satisfied a perverted urge.'

Cain pushed back his chair and got up.

'I'll send the fingerprint people along to see what they can find on your kitchen window and the fire escape.'

'I'm almost sure he was wearing gloves.'

'We'll check, anyway. And may I suggest, Miss Epton, that you lock your kitchen window before going to bed, however hot the night? Buy a fan instead.' He glanced up at the wall clock. 'Six o'clock and I already feel I've done a full day's work.'

'It's good practice for when you have a crying baby in the house.'

'Not long to go now,' he said with a surprisingly contented smile. 'Well, I'll be off. I'll let you know as soon as we've found Kirby.'

'I'll be even more interested to hear who Dieter is.'

'I'll let you know that, too.'

Chapter 28

Somehow Rosa got through the morning in court. Fortunately the case in which she was appearing was straightforward. By the time she returned to the office, however, she felt ready to collapse. It wasn't the shortage of sleep so much as the delayed reaction to the night's events. She didn't want to talk to anyone about her experience, though she knew this would be what a psychologist would recommend. She simply told Stephanie that she wasn't feeling very well and thought she would go home.

'You've probably picked up a virus,' Stephanie remarked. 'I'll tell Mr Snaith when he comes in. Anything else you'd like me to do?'

'No thanks, Steph. I'll hope to be back tomorrow.'

Stephanie nodded and turned back to the switchboard while Rosa made her escape.

As soon as she reached home, she made a cup of tea, took an analgesic tablet and went and lay down. She decided that she was probably suffering from mild shock in the aftermath of events. She was sure, however, that hot tea, the analgesic tablet and a few hours' rest would bring her back to normal. Happily, the weather had turned cooler and a fresh breeze ruffled her bedroom curtains. She had given a small shiver when she opened the window, but it was a sheer fifty-foot drop to the ground below and, anyway, she couldn't spend the rest of her life in sealed rooms.

She awoke from a dreamless sleep with a mild headache, but otherwise all right. She glanced at her bedside clock and saw that four hours had passed since she flopped out. A few minutes later the phone rang and she roused herself to go and answer it.

'Rosa?' said an anxious voice.

'Hello, Peter. When did you get back?'

'I'm at Heathrow now. I called the office and Stephanie said you weren't well and had gone home. What's wrong?'

'I'm better now. I've had a good sleep.'

'Have you phoned the doctor?'

'No, that's not necessary. But I want to talk to somebody.'

'Who?'

'Anybody,' she said with a slight note of hysteria, 'but you in particular.'

'Stay where you are and I'll be with you very soon.'

By the time Peter arrived, Rosa had taken a shower and got dressed.

'What's happened?' he asked, with a worried expression as soon as she opened the front door. Before she had time to make a coherent reply, however, he had clasped her in his arms and was kissing her.

'Colin Kirby broke into my flat when I was in bed last night,' she said, when he released her from his embrace. At that moment she burst into tears.

It was a while before she could speak, but then under Peter's soothing influence she told him the whole story.

When she finished he stared at her incredulously, apparently bereft of speech.

Eventually words came to him and he said, 'To think while this was going on, I was trying to persuade a client to invest his millions in works of art.' Wrapping his arms around her again, he added, 'A Rubens or a Rosa, I know which I'd sooner have.'

189

Rosa broke into laughter and immediately felt better for it.

'I wonder how long it'll take them to find Kirby?' Peter said.

'And whether he'll be alive or dead?'

'You think he might kill himself?'

'I'd say it's a distinct possibility. Somebody who holds other people's lives so cheaply wouldn't shrink from taking his own once he'd seen the alternative.' She gave Peter a rueful smile and went on, 'I'm glad I never liked him. It'll make it easier to get over what's happened, I'm sure of that.'

'There's something else I'm sure of. If you have another intruder in your room tonight it won't be Kirby.'

Ten days passed before Rosa heard anything further from Chief Inspector Cain. By then she had made up her mind that Colin Kirby had disappeared as completely as Lord Lucan some fifteen years earlier. She thought it quite possible that no trace of him would ever be found, not because he had acquired a fresh identity and found refuge in a remote part of South America, but because he had committed suicide much closer to hand. If you are sufficiently determined, it isn't difficult to kill yourself and ensure that your body is never likely to be found. You could jump heavily weighted into a harbour; crawl into the back of a secluded cave and shoot yourself; or take an overdose of sleeping tablets in the shelter of a forest. In all these instances, the chances of discovery would be negligible. Moreover, given a few months, there wouldn't be much left of you, anyway. Merely a few bones.

She was surprised, therefore, to receive a call from Cain in the middle of the second week after Kirby had vanished.

'We've found him, Miss Epton,' he announced with a mild note of triumph.

'Alive?'

'Just about. He'd been living rough in a deserted crofter's

cottage in the wilds of Inverness. A keen-eyed naturalist, who was out with his binoculars, spotted him going in and out of the cottage, which he knew was unoccupied. He mentioned it to the local bobby who decided to investigate. He found Kirby asleep. He'd grown a beard and refused to say who he was. Indeed, he refused to speak at all, though he eventually agreed to accompany the officer who decided to drive him to the local hospital, believing he had a nutcase on his hands. And, anyway, as far as he was concerned the man hadn't committed any crime for which he could be held in custody. The officer had the good sense to take possession of the man's clothing in the hope of identifying him. In his wallet, there was a driving licence and a bank card, both in the name of Colin Kirby. Leaving Kirby at the hospital, he went back to his station and spoke to his headquarters. As you can imagine, it wasn't very long before all the lines were humming.'

'Have you seen Kirby yourself?' Rosa broke in.

'Yes. Sergeant Saddler and I brought him back to London yesterday.'

'Is he all right?'

'Physically, yes. Mentally . . . Well, let me say you wouldn't want him to escort you out for an evening.'

'I wouldn't have, anyway. Has he talked?'

'A great deal. I think it was a reaction to hot, sweet tea and familiar faces. Also he hadn't spoken to anyone for ten days. He said he'd gone up to Scotland, fully intending to do away with himself somewhere he'd never be found, but with each day that passed, his determination weakened.'

'Has he admitted the murders?'

'Yes, but in an almost off-hand manner. He said that Ruding and Gillfroy didn't deserve to live. He deposited Ruding's body outside the prison to confuse the police and Gillfroy's on top of Eddie's grave because, as he put it, they were birds of a feather.'

'Sounds as if he's gone over the edge.'

Cain sighed. 'Ultimately, that'll be for a court to decide.'

191

'Will you be dropping the case against Grigg?'

Cain sighed anew. 'I'm afraid so. But with luck, his number will soon come up again. If not for murder, at least for something that carries a nice long sentence. Well, that's about it, Miss Epton, but I'll be in touch. We may need you as a witness.'

'And what about Dieter?' Rosa said. 'Have you discovered who he is or was?'

'I wondered if you were going to ask,' Cain said lightly. 'It seems that Kirby used to nip over to Amsterdam for naughty weekends. One of his favourite haunts was a certain male brothel where they knew him as Dieter. Nobody uses his own name in those establishments.'

'I should have guessed it was something like that.'

'You can't expect to be right about everything, Miss Epton.'

'I suppose the foreign intelligence service that approached him in Amsterdam knew about his visits to the brothel.'

'I believe', Cain observed drily, 'that they're quite a fruitful source of information to the world's spymasters.'